DOCTOR AT SEA

By the author of

Doctor in

the House

Doctor at Sea

RICHARD GORDON

London
MICHAEL JOSEPH

First published by
MICHAEL JOSEPH LTD.
26 *Bloomsbury Street*
*London, W.C.*1

FEBRUARY 1953
SECOND IMPRESSION BEFORE PUBLICATION
THIRD IMPRESSION MARCH 1953
FOURTH IMPRESSION APRIL 1953
FIFTH IMPRESSION JUNE 1953
SIXTH IMPRESSION AUGUST 1953
SEVENTH IMPRESSION OCTOBER 1953
EIGHTH IMPRESSION [RE-SET] JANUARY 1954
NINTH IMPRESSION APRIL 1954
TENTH IMPRESSION JUNE 1954
ELEVENTH IMPRESSION JULY 1954
TWELFTH IMPRESSION AUGUST 1954
THIRTEENTH IMPRESSION SEPTEMBER 1954
FOURTEENTH IMPRESSION NOVEMBER 1954
FIFTEENTH IMPRESSION DECEMBER 1954
SIXTEENTH IMPRESSION JANUARY 1955

*Set and printed in Great Britain by Tonbridge Printers Ltd., Peach
Hall Works, Tonbridge, in Baskerville eleven on thirteen point, on
paper made by John Dickinson at Croxley, and bound by James
Burn at Esher*

To

THE MERCHANT NAVY

*They have a
lot to put up with*

NOTE

The *Lotus* and her crew are as
fictitious as the *Flying Dutchman*
and her insubstantial company.

1

IT would be unfair to describe the *Lotus* as an unlucky ship. It was just that she was accident prone, like a big, awkward schoolgirl.

Even her period of gestation in the shipyard was full of mishaps. She was laid down in Wallsend in 1929, and had advanced to the shape of a huge picked chicken when the depression blew down bitterly on Tyneside. For the next four years she rusted untouched behind locked gates, and when they started work again her design was changed on the drawing-board from a North Atlantic ship to a Far East trader. Shortly afterwards the company ordering her went bankrupt and she was bought on the stocks by another, who began to turn her into a whaler. They too rapidly slid into insolvency and abandoned her to a fourth, the Fathom Steamship Company of St. Mary Axe. It was this concern that succeeded in launching her, after she had been through as many fruitless changes in construction as a human embryo.

At her launch she holed and almost sunk a small tug, and on her maiden voyage as a cargo-passenger ship she lost a propeller during a gale in the Australian Bight. At the beginning of the war she came home from New Zealand, painted grey, and was one of the first vessels to reveal to the Admiralty the effectiveness of the magnetic mine. She lost most of her bows in the Thames Estuary, but stayed afloat long enough to be dragged into dock for repairs. After several months she set off again to join a convoy, and had her stern blown away by a bomb twenty-five minutes after leaving port.

The stern was patched up, and she managed to pass the rest of the hostilities without getting herself involved in any dangerous action, apart from shooting down an American Mustang in error with her Oerlikons in 1945. At the end of the war she refitted and returned to peaceful trading, disturbed only by an explosion in the engine-room in the Caribbean and the cook going abruptly insane one insupportably hot afternoon in the Red Sea and passing among his shipmates with the meat hatchet.

Much of the damage from both these accidents was repaired, but the repeated structural changes had induced in the *Lotus* a premature senility, a state of chronic invalidism. She was too cold in the higher latitudes, too hot in the Tropics, and she groaned pitifully in bad weather. But the Fathom Steamship Company unmercifully sent her anywhere in the world where she could find the shareholders a profit. She carried lead and lemons, boiler-tubes and barley, copra and cows. She took steel from Baltimore to Brisbane, wool from Auckland to Archangel, coal from Swansea to Singapore. She was one of the world's shopping baskets.

There was enough room on board for thirty passengers, though she rarely carried more than a dozen and often none at all. They were people going to unusual places, or too poor to afford a big ship, or experienced travellers who

cringed before the bonhomie of the boatdeck and the
deadly gin-and-sin routine of a sophisticated liner. The
Company was indifferent to them: passengers earned little
more than complaints, but freight meant money.

In the opinion of the crew, one of the severest disasters
to overtake the *Lotus* since the war was her Commander,
Captain Vincent Hogg, who was officially required to act
at various times once his ship was at sea as the sole repre-
sentative on board of the Fathom Steamship Company,
the King, and God, for all three of them he substituted
himself with impartial grandeur. His officers accepted him
as farmers tolerate a prolonged drought, giving daily
prayers for Divine removal of the affliction. The weight
of his personality fell most heavily on the Mate, Mr.
Hornbeam, who had passed his Master's examination
twenty years before and was waiting for a command with
the pitiful patience of an impoverished expectant relative.
Promotion in the Company was simply a matter of dead
men's shoes. He had in a drawer in his cabin an alpha-
betical list of the Fathom Line's Captains, with their exact
ages and notes on their partiality for drink, loose women,
and other items reputed to shorten life, but all of them
retained irritatingly good health. He enjoyed the unstinted sympathy of the Chief Engineer, Mr. McDougall,
who hated the Captain like a red-hot bearing; and the
Captain disliked the Chief Engineer like fog round the
Goodwins. McDougall looked upon the ship as a shell for
the transportation of his engines, and complained daily
when the navigational position from the bridge was some
miles astern of the one he calculated from his revolutions.
Indeed, according to the Chief Engineer, the machinery
and boilers of the *Lotus* should have arrived in any port
several days in advance of the rest of the vessel.

There were two other Mates, a gang of engineers, a wireless operator and—as the *Lotus* carried more than ninety-nine souls when she was full—a doctor.

The doctor was by order of the Ministry of Transport, the uncompromising power who prescribes on every item of a sailor's life from the number of lifeboats to be available in emergency to the number of times he shall have eggs for his breakfast. Ninety-eight souls can sail the seas until they are carried away with obscure nautical illnesses, like the shipmates of the Ancient Mariner: their health is preserved with a bottle of black draught, the *Ship Captain's Medical Guide*, and a scapel also used for sharpening the chart-room pencil. The Second Mate or the Chief Steward holds the keys of the drug chest and practices daily, after breakfast. All pains below the umbilicus are treated with strong purgative, all disturbances above with Ministry cough mixture, and lesions on the remainder of the body with turpentine liniment. Obviously there occur from time to time more alarming complaints, and these are submitted to surgery under wireless instructions by the Captain on the saloon table, after the patient and the surgeon have taken sufficient brandy to instil in each other confidence that both will survive the operation.

But one more soul on board brings to all the benefits of medical science—or as much of it as the doctor can remember, because ship surgeons are notoriously forgetful of these things. The sea induces an attitude of pleasant detachment towards problems that strain thought ashore, including those of the diagnosis and progress of disease, and the doctor has few professional obligations to distract him from his pastimes or enrich him with experience. For these reasons the companies naturally dislike the expense of carrying him—but then, the Fathom Steamship

Company would have objected to the expense of life-boats.

When I met the *Lotus* she was lying in Liverpool, due to sail with a cargo of machinery and motor cars to Santos, in Brazil. It had then been raining on Merseyside for four days. The damp November wind channelled itself down the river, broke against the waterfront buildings, and ran up the cold streets behind. The birds on the Liver building, that are unfairly supposed by Liverpool seafarers to flap their wings when passed by a woman of untarnished virtue, wept ceaselessly on to the bleak pierhead. The Birkenhead ferry forced its way miserably across the choppy harbour, the landing-stage looked as forlorn as a bandstand in midwinter, and even the stonework of the St. George's Hall appeared in danger of showing through its crust of soot.

It was about eight in the evening, the hour when the shipowners are fed in the Adelphi. As they glumly finished their Martinis in the little American bar they calculated among themselves the rain's cost in delayed cargo working. Outside in Lime Street the adolescent tarts already clung hopefully to their damp doorways. The dripping buses took home the last pale shipping clerks, the overhead railway rattled along its grotesque track, and the dock police steamed themselves warm in front of the stoves in their cabins. The *Lotus* herself lay lifeless at her quay with tarpaulins tented over her hatches, creaking gently at her mooring ropes like an old bed in a bad dream.

I stood in the rain on the quayside reading a large sheet of printed instructions for resuscitating the apparently drowned. This was the only information of any sort available to passers-by. The wharf was deserted. The cranes huddled together in a row, a few railway trucks crouched between their legs; the warehouses were shut, locked, and abandoned even by the cats; the *Lotus*, lit with a few dim lights, looked as uninviting as a shut pub.

I was a young doctor with a bad diploma passing through the difficult stage of professional adolescence when you discover the medical schools teach as little about medicine as the public schools do about life. My knowledge of seafaring was based only on *Treasure Island*, pictures in the windows of Cook's, and a walking-on part I had been allowed to play in a students' production of *The Middle Watch*. I was nevertheless a recognized sailor. I had in my pocket a new seaman's identity card with my fingerprints on it, a document that made me the professional descendant of Drake and Cabot, subject to and protected by a batch of Parliamentary Acts, the target of missionaries' good intentions and girls' bad ones, and entitled, if I felt like it and there was enough room, to doss down in the Sailors' Home.

The first problem presented by nautical life was how to get aboard the ship. A slippery gangway reached up from the wharf to the *Lotus's* afterdeck, but there was no one to welcome me at the top. After a few damp minutes I climbed the gangway nervously and looked around me. I was on a dirty iron deck littered with pieces of timber, scraps of rope, and coils of wire, like the junk room in a ship chandler's. A heavy wooden door led into the upper works, and as the rain was coming down my neck persistently I opened it and stepped inside.

Hostile darkness surrounded me; I smelt the faint bitter-almonds tang of cyanide. Uneasy tales of the sea blew through my mind, like a sudden cold draught in an old house. It occurred to me that the *Lotus*, like the *Marie*

Celeste, had been freshly abandoned by her terrified crew,
or was manned with lost souls from the *Flying Dutchman*.
I shivered.

A light, an oil lantern, sprung into mid air in front of
me. A voice behind it snapped:

' 'Op it!'

I jumped back, hitting the door with my head.

'Get the 'ell out of it, Charlie,' the voice continued,
coming nearer.

'I—I'm a member of the crew,' I managed to say.

The light advanced on me. Behind it two eyes stared
with concentrated suspicion.

'The new doctor,' I explained humbly.

The voice at once took on a friendly inflection.

'Sorry, Doc! I thought you was trying to pinch something.'

'No . . . I just came aboard. There didn't seem to be
anyone about. I hope it was all right?'

'Sure, it's all right. Liberty Hall, this hooker. Make
yourself at home. Spit on the deck and call the cat a
bastard.'

'Thank you.'

'Glad you've come, Doc,' he continued affably. 'I've
got a bit of a cold, like.' He sneezed to add point to the
remark. 'Could you give us something for it?'

'Yes, certainly . . . But wouldn't a bit later do? I'm
extremely wet. I'd like to find my cabin and so forth.'

'Sure, Doc. Follow me. I'll take you to see the
Mate.'

He walked off, the lamp swinging high in his hand.
I stepped timidly behind him, along narrow alleyways,
round sharp corners, up unidentifiable ladders.

'Sorry there ain't many lights,' he apologized over his

shoulder. 'But the engineers has got the jennies stripped to-night.'

'Oh, really?'

That sounded more alarming than ever.

He came to a cabin door and opened it.

'The new Doctor,' he announced, as if he had just materialized me out of a hat.

There were three men in the cabin—the Mate, Archer the Second, and Trail the Third. Hornbeam was sitting in the only chair with his reefer unbuttoned and his stockinged feet on the washbasin. It was a small cabin, designed like a crossword puzzle, and the visitors had to adopt themselves to the interlocking pieces. Archer, who was a tall, pale man with an expression like a curate just beginning to have doubts, had wedged himself between the bunk and the bookcase above it with his legs dangling on to the deck, like a human question mark. Trail, squatting between the locker and the desk, was a fat youth going through a florid attack of *acne vulgaris*.

'Talk of the devil!' Hornbeam said immediately.

'We wondered when you were going to turn up,' Archer said. 'Have a bottle of beer.'

'Move over, Second, and let the Doctor park his fanny,' Hornbeam said. He introduced himself and the others. 'Give us another bottle, Third. Do you mind drinking out of a tooth-glass?'

'No, not at all.'

The welcome was cordial enough, but it disturbed me. It is a habit among seafarers to accept every newcomer on terms of intimacy, but I was a fairly new doctor and stood on my professional dignity like a girl with her first pair of high heels.

'I hope I'm not butting in,' I said stiffly.

'Not a bit of it! Throw your coat on the hook there. We were only having a quick peg.'

I climbed up on the bunk next to Archer without enthusiasm. It seemed as comfortable as trying to drink on a bus in the rush hour.

'You just passed out of medical school?' Archer asked.

'Certainly not! I've been in practice for . . . some years.'

'Oh, sorry. Been to sea before?'

'I'm afraid not.'

'You'll soon pick up the routine. I hope you're hot stuff on the diseases sailors get.'

This brought a roar of laughter from the other two.

'We doctors have to be "hot stuff" on very many things,' I said.

I gave a superior smile. Since I qualified I had fed on professional respect and I found the conversation irritating.

'By George, we find some queer doctors at sea,' Trail said, handing me a glass of beer. 'Don't we, Mr. Horn-beam? Usually they're getting away from their wives or the police, or both sometimes. Or else it's drink. That's the commonest. Sometimes it's drugs, though.'

'I drink very little.'

Trail took no notice. 'I remember old Doc Parsons I sailed with when I was doing my time,' he went on cheerfully. 'He was a real scream. As tight as a tick from morning to night. We reckoned he got through a couple of bottles of gin a day, easy. Started before breakfast, every morning. Said the world was so bloody awful he couldn't face it at the best of times, but especially with his last night's hangover. Then one day in the Red Sea the Mate ripped his arm open, and old Parsons said he'd operate. Laugh! The lot of us went down to the hospital to watch.

I was doubled up. He'd been at the bottle extra strong and he was as blind as a bat. Kept dropping the knife on the deck and falling over the table. In the end the Mate clocked him one and got the Chief Steward to do it.'

Archer leant forward.

'Do you remember old Doc Hamilton in the *Mariesta?*' he asked.

The other two began to laugh again.

'He was a real queer 'un,' he explained to me. 'Started on the grog before we sailed—had to be carried up the gangway. By the time we reached Gib. the Old Man stopped his tap—no more booze, you understand. So he went down to the dispensary and drank all the surgical spirit. When he finished that he scrounged meths from the engineers. They tumbled to it, of course, and wouldn't let him have any more. In the end he drank the acid from the wireless batteries.'

'The police came for him when we got home,' Hornbeam added. 'I don't know what it was for. Something about abortions, I think.'

'I remember we buried an old doctor off Teneriffe,' Archer said thoughtfully. 'He hanged himself. He did it with his belt,' he continued in my direction.

I began to understand that the medical professional was not held in the highest esteem at sea.

'I assure you I shall not commit any of those things,' I said.

'The voyage hasn't started yet,' Archer observed. 'Why, look what happened to old Doc Flowerday.'

'Yes, that was a shame,' Trail said, nodding his head sadly. 'He was as mad as you make 'em. But I was sorry about it, for one.'

Hornbeam agreed.

'He was a nice old boy. You heard all about it, I suppose, Doc?'

'No, I haven't. Why? Should I?'

He suddenly looked uncomfortable.

'I thought they might have told you something about it in the office,' he said vaguely. 'He was the last doctor before you.'

He sighed gently into his beer.

'It was a pity,' he continued. 'In a way.'

I shifted myself nervously on the bunk.

'What was a pity?'

Hornbeam drained his glass.

'His . . . well, his end, as you might say.'

They sat in silence for a while. The reference to Dr. Flowerday had saddened them, and no one seemed to wish to reopen the conversation. I sat and anxiously speculated on his possible fate, for which I had now a good number of workable theories.

2

I WENT to bed that night feeling like my first day at school when someone pinched my tuck-box. But in the morning the rain had stopped and the sun threw a bloodshot early glance on Merseyside. The ship had come to life overnight. She rattled with the noise of steam winches loading cargo, and the ghosts of the evening were replaced by persons who shouted, coughed, and used bad language on each other with comforting humanity.

I had breakfast in the saloon with Hornbeam and the Mates. Their conversation was as mysterious to me as the chat at the hospital lunch-table would have been to them: it was about 'tween decks and stowage, dunnage and ullage, tank tops and cofferdams. The only fact I could grasp was that the *Lotus's* sailing date was as unpredictable as Judgment Day.

After breakfast I went to my cabin, sat on the narrow strip of settee, and opened the first page of *War and Peace*. This I had bought in three volumes from a bookseller's near Euston Station before catching the train for Liverpool. I thought the voyage would allow me to achieve a ten-year's ambition of finishing the thing; besides, I was

determined to make use of the time I was obliged to spend
inactively at sea improving my mind. And its long,
restful paragraphs might begin to soothe my headaches.

A fortnight ago I had been an assistant in general
practice—the medical equivalent of the poor curate,
the unbriefed barrister, the new subaltern—living in an
atmosphere of Dettol and damp overcoats and dispensing
the loot of the National Health Service like a maniacal
Lady Bountiful. My principal had a bedside manner and
two stock remedies with which he had built up a local
reputation of infallibility, and we divided the work
between us. He saw the private patients, who diminished
in number each Budget day, and took the morning
surgery; I had the night calls and the evening clinic. As my
clinic came conveniently after work, school, and high tea,
it was popular with everyone who wanted a certificate,
new teeth, hair, or spectacles, or simply to pass the time.
The patients brought their troubles and left them on my
doorstep like unwanted babies. They wedged themselves
into the uncomfortable and unhygienic-looking sofas in our
waiting-room, mirthlessly turning the pages of *Punch*, and
glancing shiftily at their neighbours wondering what they
had got and if it was catching. There were so many of
them they could idle the drab hours of their evening away
contentedly. It was cheaper than the pub, and more
interesting.

For this I was paid the same wages as an engine-driver;
in ten or fifteen years, however, if I behaved myself, I
would become a partner and take a share in the spoils.
But my life at the time was illuminated with a more
pressing excitement: I was going to get married.

Marriage is as much of an obligation for a young
doctor as celibacy for a Roman Catholic priest. A medical

bachelor is unpopular with the patients, except for visits to eligible daughters, and as even these are now obtainable on the National Health he is a frank financial liability to the practice. My principal had no intention of losing his patients through marital hesitation on the part of his young assistant, and after he had made this as plain as possible he asked his wife to apply a woman's practical mind to the problem and set about finding me a bride.

She procured the daughter of a town councillor. She was a girl called Wendy, a blonde, but of the arid sort, like the stubble in a wheatfield after a hot harvest. Her position in local society made it impossible for me to escape: once the town saw what my principal's wife was up to, Wendy and I were mated as firmly as two rats put in the same cage in the biological laboratory.

We became engaged. The wedding approached with the speed of an early winter.

I suppose, looking back on it, there was good reason for my subconscious to slip into disorder, like a wrecked gear-box in an overdriven car. Wendy was a nice girl. She was well educated, and could talk about things like trigonometry and economics. But she had her defects. Her voice was as dull and authoritative as a Salvation Army drum, she walked like an overloaded wheelbarrow, and she had a figure like a stook of corn. I began to suffer an attack of *terror celebans*, or bachelor's panic.

More robust personalities than mine would have stood up to it: it is a common premarital complaint. But I did not. I developed headaches. I immediately diagnosed a cerebral tumour and hurried to London to see a brain specialist, savouring everything on the way with exquisite farewell tenderness, even the fish served for lunch by British Railways.

The brain specialist listened to me for five minutes and packed me off to a psychiatrist. The psychiatrist was an important and busy man and I arrived at the end of the day, but he let me talk for a quarter of an hour while he signed a few letters and looked for his car key.

'A long holiday,' he said sternly, putting on his overcoat. 'Why don't you take a ship? You won't have any work to do. I did it when I was your age. Signed on a cattle boat going to Murmansk. Half the deckhands were washed overboard one night and I had to turn-to with the rest of them to work the ship. Great fun.'

'I don't think I'd be much good as a deckhand.'

'Anyway, you've got to have a holiday. Put on your best suit and walk down Leadenhall Street. You never know your luck.'

'All right, sir,' I said doubtfully. 'If you advise.'

Thus my honour was saved by modern psychiatry.

The next afternoon I tramped Leadenhall Street, trying to get a berth out of every big shipping office and, by mistake, a branch of Barclay's Bank. It was one of those unfriendly November days when dawn and dusk meet each other in a dim conspiracy over the lunch-table. The rain drizzled on to the grimy pavements, soaking through my mackintosh and the seams of my shoes, and my depression deepened with the twilight. It looked as if the sea had rejected me.

When the offices began to close and the important shipping men were already hurrying westwards I walked up the creaking stairs of the Fathom Line building, prepared to sail with Captain Bligh if necessary. There I was introduced to a Mr. Cozens, a little bald man crouched in a high leather chair. He was suspiciously pleased to see me.

'Our *Lotus*, Doctor,' he said, 'is in need of a surgeon. We should be delighted to have you. Forty pounds a month, no need for uniform, just the Company's regulation cap. Can you leave for Santos on Monday?'

But a seafaring friend had once warned me to treat a new ship like a prospective bride and discover her exact age and precise tonnage before committing myself. And I was touchy on such points.

Cozens rapidly sketched for me a description of the *Lotus*. 'She isn't a *big* ship,' he concluded. 'Nor a *fast* ship, exactly.' He smiled like a house agent. 'But she's a very *nice* ship.'

I wondered what to do. I was being asked to sail in a ship I had never seen, to a place I had never heard of, in the employ of a business I knew nothing about. I looked anxiously through the dark window running with comforting English rain. The wisest course was obviously to go back to Wendy and settle for a fortnight in Sidmouth instead.

'Very well,' I said. 'I accept.'

'Excellent!' said Mr. Cozens, with relief. 'I'm sure you'll find yourself well suited, Doctor. She's a very nice ship indeed. Quite a lady.'

I nodded. 'Where do I go now?'

'There are a few formalities to be gone through I'm afraid, Doctor. Regulations and such things, you understand. First of all, I must supply you with a letter of appointment. If you'll just wait one minute I'll get one of the girls to type it.'

Running away to sea has become more elaborate since the unhedged days when the errant son slipped down to the docks at nightfall, mated up with a bos'n at a wharf-side tavern, and sailed with an Indiaman on the dawn tide. Now there are forms to be filled in, documents to be issued, permits to be warily exchanged for a string of personal data. The next day I was sent down to the Merchant Navy Office, an establishment which was a cross between a railway booking-hall and the charge-room of a police station on a Saturday night. There I poked my letter of appointment nervously through a small window at a clerk, who glanced through it with the unconcealed disgust of a post office employee reading one's private thoughts in a telegram.

'Got your lifeboat ticket?' he asked gloomily, his steel nib arrested in mid-air.

'My what?' I saw for a second the picture of myself shivering on a sinking deck, refused permission to enter the lifeboat because I had not purchased my ticket at the proper counter. 'Where do I buy it?' I asked wildly.

The man looked at me with pity. 'They sends us some mugs these days,' he observed wearily. 'Lifeboat ticket,' he repeated, mouthing the words as if addressing a deaf idiot. 'Ministry certificate. Savvy?'

'No,' I admitted. 'I haven't.'

'Got any distinguishing marks?' he asked, giving me a chance to redeem myself. 'Or blemishes? Tattoos?'

'No. None at all. As far as I know.'

He nodded and gave me a chit entitling me to a free photograph at a shop across the street. I queued between a tall negro in a jacket that half covered his thighs and a man in a strong-smelling roll-necked sweater who picked his teeth with a safety-pin. When my turn came I had to face the camera holding my number in a wooden frame under my chin, and I felt the next step would be in handcuffs.

Now, sitting in my cabin with *War and Peace*, my

Company's Regulation Cap hanging from a hook above me, I saw that Mr. Cozens was wrong. The *Lotus* wasn't a nice ship at all. She was a floating warehouse, with some accommodation for humans stuck on top like a watchman's attic. All the cabins were small, and mine was like a railway compartment quarter-filled with large pipes. I wondered where they went to, and later discovered I was situated immediately below the Captain's lavatory.

My appraisal of the *Lotus* was interrupted by a knock on the jalousie door. It was Easter, the Doctor's steward. He was a little globular man, who felt his position was not that of a mere servant but of a slightly professional gentleman. As an indication of his superiority to his messmates a throat torch and a thermometer poked out of the top pocket of his jacket, and he frequently talked to me about 'We of the medical fraternity.' He was always ready to give advice to his companions on problems of a medical or social nature that they felt disinclined to pour into the ears of the Doctor, and had an annoying habit of counselling them, for the good of their health, to hurl into the sea the bottles of physic just handed to them by their medical attendant.

'Good morning, Doctor,' he said. 'I have a message from Father.'

'Father?'

'The Captain.'

'Oh.'

'He said he wants a bottle of his usual stomach mixture, pronto.'

'His usual stomach mixture?' I took off my spectacles and frowned. 'How do I know what that is? Has he got a prescription, or anything?'

'Dr. Flowerday used to make him up a bottle special.'

'I see.'

The problem grew in importance the more I thought of it.

'The Captain suffers from his stomach quite frequently, does he?'

'Ho, yes, sir. Something chronic.'

'Hm.'

'When he has one of his spasms he gets a cob on, worse than usual. Life ain't worth living for all hands. The only stuff what squares up his innards is the special mixture he got from Dr. Flowerday. Makes him bring up the wind, Doctor. Or belch, as we say in the medical profession.'

'Quite. You don't know what's in this medicine, I suppose?'

'Not the foggiest, Doctor.'

'Well, can't you remember? You were with Dr. Flowerday some time, weren't you?'

'Several voyages, Doctor. And he was very satisfied, if I may make so bold.'

It occurred to me that this might be the point to clear up the Flowerday mystery for good.

'Tell me, Easter,' I said sharply, 'what exactly happened to Dr. Flowerday?'

He scratched his nose with a sad gesture.

'If you wouldn't mind, sir,' he replied with dignity, 'I'd rather not talk about it.'

I got up. It was useless sounding Easter on the fate of my predecessor or on his balm for the Captain's gastric disorders.

Down aft there was a cabin with a notice stencilled above the door saying CERTIFIED HOSPITAL. It was a fairly large apartment which smelt like an underground cell that hadn't been used for some time. There

were four cots in it, in a couple of tiers. One bulkhead was
taken up with a large locker labelled in red POISONS,
one door of which was lying adrift of its hinges on the
deck.

Inside the locker were half a dozen rows of square,
squat bottles containing the supply of medicines for the
ship. These—like the Doctor—were prescribed by the
Ministry of Transport. Unfortunately the Ministry, in
the manner of the elderly, elegant physicians who come
monthly out of retirement to grace the meetings of the
Royal Society of Medicine, holds trustingly to the old-
established remedies and the comely prescriptions of
earlier decades. There were drugs in the cupboard that I
had seen only in out-of-date books on pharmacology. I
picked up a bottle: *Amylum*. What on earth did one do with
amylum? There was a pound of Dover's powder and a
drum of castor oil big enough to move the bowels of
the earth. At the back I found an empty gin bottle,
some Worcester sauce, a tennis racket with broken
strings, a dirty pair of black uniform socks, two eggs,
a copy of the *Brisbane Telegraph*, and a notice saying NO
FUMARE.

I dropped these through the porthole, taking care with
the eggs. Below the shelves of bottles was another compartment. I looked into it. It held a heavy mahogany case
labelled INSTRUMENT CHEST, which contained the
left component of a pair of obstetrical forceps, a saw, a
bottle-opener, and a bunch of tooth-picks; but there were
five gross of grey cardboard eyeshades, over seven apiece
for all hands.

I saw that prescribing was going to be more difficult
than in general practice, where I scribbled a prescription
on my pad and the patient took it to the chemist, who

deciphered my writing and slickly made up the medicine. We had been obliged to attend a course of lectures on pharmacy and dispensing in medical school, but these were always held on a Saturday morning, when most of the students were already on their way to the rugger field. For this reason there was an informal roster among the class to forge the signatures of their companions on the attendance sheet, before slipping softly away themselves when the lecturer turned to clarify some obscure pharmacological point on the blackboard. As I had attended the greater number of my pharmacy lectures by proxy in this way, I now felt like a new wife in her first kitchen.

I picked up one or two bottles hopefully, and I was delighted to find that my predecessor, Dr. Flowerday, had his pharmacy lectures on Saturday mornings also. On the back of each bottle was a small label bearing in shaky handwriting guidance such as 'Good for diarrhœa,' or 'This mixed with Tinct. Ipecac. seems all right for colds,' or 'Apparently inert.' There was also a sheet of cardboard on which Dr. Flowerday had written in Portuguese, Spanish, French, and Hindustani translations of three questions which he seemed to find adequate for investigating his patients: 'Have you a cough?' 'Where is the pain?' and 'Have you been with any dirty women recently?'

I found an old pair of pharmacist's scales and a glass graduated in drachms, and started to make up the Captain's medicine. The first one turned into a pink putty, and was abandoned (it later came in useful for minor infections of the crew's feet). The second tasted strongly of peppermint but seemed adequate. I corked it and carried it up to the Captain's cabin.

I had not met Captain Hogg before. He had been ashore the previous night and he never came down for breakfast. When I had asked Hornbeam about him he replied unconvincingly, 'He has his good points.'

'What are they?' Trail asked gloomily.

I enquired what form Captain Hogg's malignity took.

'Oh, he thinks the sun shines out of his bottom,' Trail said. 'They all get like that. It's living alone too much that does it. They ought to be made to carry their wives with them to keep them under control.'

'The Old Man isn't married,' Hornbeam told him.

'Neither was his father,' Trail said.

I knocked on the cabin door.

'Enter!'

I went in.

Captain Hogg was of a curious shape. He was like a huge pear. From the sharp top of his bald head he came out gradually until the region of the umbilicus, from which point he spread abruptly in all directions. He was sitting in an armchair in his shirt-sleeves, his face obscured by the book he was reading. It was a periodical called *True Horrors*, on the front of which a vivid blonde with an alarming bosom was struggling unsuccessfully with a gorilla, a man in a black mask, and her under-clothes.

The book didn't move. I stood just inside the door, holding the medicine bottle in front of me like a talisman. He spoke:

'Well?'

I rubbed my right shoe slowly up my left calf.

'Doctor, sir,' I said.

The magazine came down. For a moment we stared at

each other with interest. I thought he looked as friendly as
a firing-squad.

'Ah!' he said.

I proffered the bottle.

'Your stomach mixture, sir.'

Either my prescribing or Dr. Flowerday's directions
were at fault; perhaps the ship's drugs had degenerated
with time. Some unplanned reaction occurred within the
bottle. With a sharp pop the cork flew into the air.

'You may find this a little strong,' I said, picking up the
cork quickly. 'I recommend taking it well diluted.'

He took the bottle silently and stood it on the desk
beside him.

'Your cap,' he said. 'You have a cap?'

'Yes, sir. Company's regulation pattern.'

'Why aren't you wearing it?'

'I'm sorry sir, I——'

'The cap is worn on all official visits to the Captain.
If I were asking you up here for a peg, that would be
different. But I'm not. It's a matter of etiquette. There's
no tramp ship stuff about this vessel. This is my ship, you
understand, Doctor? *My* ship. If we get that straight we
shall rub along splendidly together.'

'Yes, sir.'

I was a medical student again, before the Dean for
filling the senior surgeon's rubber operating boots with
iced water.

'Good. You haven't been to sea before?'

'No, sir.'

'You'll find the routine fairly simple, as far as you're
concerned. You take your surgery at nine every morning,
and at ten you bring me up a list of the sick on board and
what's wrong with 'em. There's none of this damn medical

secrecy nonsense at sea. I want to know all about them. I have to carry the can in the end. Understand?'

'Yes, sir.'

'Good. Then at eleven o'clock we inspect the ship—you wear your cap again. Dinner is at twelve-thirty and supper at six. Do you play cribbage?'

'No, sir.'

He looked disappointed.

'Pity. The last Doctor played a good hand. Passes the tedium of the evenings at sea.' He indicated the magazine. 'I'm a great reading man myself, but I like a game of crib now and then.'

On a sudden thought he leant over and rummaged in the desk.

'I've got a book on it here. Read that through, then we might be able to have a few games.'

'Thank you, sir.'

He hesitated a moment, staring at the square toes of his shoes.

'Did you know Dr. Flowerday?' he asked.

'No, sir.'

'He was the last Doctor. Very good man. We all liked him very much. Unfortunately, he didn't know when to stop. I shouldn't like to see you go the same way. The Company might think there was something wrong with my ship.'

My mouth went dry.

'What—er, what happened to him, sir?'

Captain Hogg glanced at me, then returned to inspecting his toes.

'Of course, a man's entitled to think what he likes,' he said forcefully. 'I'm a respecter of anyone's opinions. But there are limits, Doctor. Limits.'

'Yes, sir.'

'You've never thought you were somebody else, for instance? Have you, Doctor?'

'No, sir. I—I can't recall doing so.'

'Well, there you are. It happens sometimes at sea. I've seen some of the best of fellows get taken that way. I remember when I first went Mate, the Third thought he was Cleopatra. Very awkward it was for all hands.'

'I can see it would be, sir.'

'But Dr. Flowerday had a weakness. I tell you in strict confidence, Doctor.'

'Of course, sir.'

It appeared that my predecessor, after having drunk two bottles of gin a day for several years in the service of the *Lotus*, got religion shortly after leaving Singapore, and extinguished himself one night in the Indian Ocean through the mistaken impression that he had the rightful ability to walk upon the water.

3

THE *Lotus* sailed, to the surprise of her crew, three days later. We spent the time tethered to the quay, loading heavy packing-cases from railway trucks. It was an interesting performance. The cases were raised to the level of the ship's deck, drawn horizontally inwards, and lowered into the holds. This was done with the derricks and steam winches, each set manned by a gang of Liverpool dockers, who went about their work with the leisurely decorum of the House of Lords considering an unimportant Bill on a hot afternoon.

There was a docker at each winch, and the rest of them worked either down the hold or on the quay. Each gang was controlled by a man in a long overcoat and a bowler hat, who directed their activities with the economy of gesture of an experienced bidder at an auction. The twitch of a little finger, an inclination of the head, the drop of an eyelid, and four tons of crated machinery went spinning through the air and down the hatch as cleanly as a holed-out golf ball.

The stowage of the cargo was supervised by the Mates, under the directions of Archer. He had his bunk covered with cargo manifests, bills of lading, and plans of the ship with the different merchandise coloured in with crayon.

'The Second gets the thin end of it,' he said. 'He's always cargo officer. Too much work in it for me.'

'But it looks fairly simple. Don't you just go on putting the stuff in until the ship's full?'

'Haven't you ever packed a case for a holiday? The things you want first always seem to be at the bottom. If that happened in the ship there'd be trouble. You can't tip everything out.'

'I see what you mean.'

'Besides, there's the trim of the ship to think about. There's more in cargo than meets the eye.'

He looked at his plan. 'Nos. 1 and 4 are full, but there's plenty of room in 2 and 3. We'll be here a week yet, you can bet on that.'

But orders, based on some deep calculation in the Fathom Line offices, came for us to sail. Twenty-four hours later, in the morning, the *Lotus* left.

An air of excitement spread through the ship before sailing, as everyone began to go about their jobs more briskly. I was greatly stimulated by the promising departure, for I had become thoroughly used to living alongside the wharf in the past few days and occasionally doubted that we would ever sail at all. The dockers who had made free with our decks were turned down the gangway, leaving behind them a litter of newspapers, cigarette packets, and matches trampled into the rusty steel. The wide hatches were covered with heavy slabs of wood, and square tarpaulins lashed over them. At the head of the gangway the quartermaster fixed a blackboard announcing confidently THE S.S. LOTUS WILL SAIL

AT 10 O'CLOCK FOR SANTOS NO SHORE LEAVE,
and a thin black stream of smoke shot powerfully upwards
from the funnel. Our bleak masts were enlivened with
flags: the red ensign trailed over our stern, the Company's
house-flag—a red F topped by an anchor on a white
square—was hoisted at the mainmast, and from the foremast the blue-and-white P announced our intentions to the
waterside.

'That at least is a flag I recognize,' I said to Trail. 'The
Blue Peter.'

'Yes, we'll soon be on our way, Doc. It's a bloody
nuisance. I was just getting a nice little piece lined up last
night. It's always the same.'

'I shall be glad to get to sea, I must say. I've seen enough
of Liverpool.'

'You'll get your bellyful of sea all right, don't you
worry. Shouldn't get too excited, though. They may
change their minds and send us into Cardiff when we get
out in the Irish Sea. Not a bad place, Cardiff, though I
prefer Middlesbrough myself. The pubs are better.'

Shortly afterwards Trail reappeared on deck with his
cap on, looking very determined and ten years older.

'Got to do the testing,' he explained brusquely. 'Tugs'll
be here any minute now.'

I heard him ring the bridge telegraphs and sound the
whistle, which blew a long silent plume of steam into the
air for some seconds before it struck its note. The customs
officers gave us a final suspicious look and made for the
shore, their threatening bags of rummage tools over their
shoulders. Men in yellow raincoats and misshapen trilbys
hurried aboard with desperate last letters addressed to
Captain Hogg, and rushed away again anxiously looking
at their watches. A Mr. Swithinbank, a pale youth with

steel spectacles from the Liverpool office, came breathlessly down the deck after me, with a paper in his
hand.

'Here's the Bill of Health, Doctor,' he said. 'Cripes! For
a moment I thought I'd lost you! You can't sail without
it.'

'Thank you very much,' I said, taking the document
reverently.

'Are you all right?' he asked quickly, making for the
gangway. 'Medical stores O.K.? Too late now, anyway.
Have a good voyage. Cheery-bye!'

'Good-bye,' I shouted after him helplessly. 'We seem a
bit short of sulphonamides.'

'Bring us a ham from Brazil if you remember it,' he
called over his shoulder. 'Don't forget the poor starving
English.'

He hurried away between the railway waggons and
lorries on the quay. It was almost ten. Two sailors, who
had somehow managed to drink themselves to a standstill
at that hour, staggered up the gangway and collapsed on
the deck.

'Take 'em below,' Hornbeam shouted to the Bos'n,
with the air of a man handling a familiar situation.
'They'll be logged to-morrow morning. Has Smiley turned
up yet?'

'No sign, Mr. Hornbeam.'

'I dunno,' Hornbeam said resignedly. 'If you docked a
ship in Hell you'd still get deserters. Get my watch turned-
to, Bos'n. I'm going to stations.'

'Aye aye, sir.'

Two tugs nuzzled under our bow and stern, their
skippers standing impassively at the wheel in their oilskins
like waiting taxi-drivers. The pilot came aboard—an

alarmingly unnautical figure in a tweed overcoat and
bowler hat, carrying an umbrella and a black Gladstone
bag. I watched Trail knock on the Captain's door, salute,
and announce 'Tugs alongside and pilot aboard, sir.' He
stepped aside as Captain Hogg appeared, resplendent
in gold braid, and mounted solemnly to the bridge. The
gangway came up, the two tugs plucked the ship away
from the quay, and the ropes fell into the water with
long splashes. The *Lotus* became suddenly changed into
an entity, a being in her own right, instead of a rusty
appendage of a dirty Liverpool wharf.

I leant over the rail with Easter, watching the steadily
widening gap of water between us and the shore. I had
never been on a moving ship before, apart from a brief
passage from Margate to Southend in a paddle steamer,
and I felt excited and apprehensive. I found the belief that
we should now all be transported by the *Lotus* from
Liverpool to the Tropics too outlandish to take seriously.

'Well, we're off,' was all I could think to say.

'Yes, sir. In an hour or so we'll be well out in the
River.'

'You know, Easter, to me it seems almost impossible for
this little ship to take us all the way to South America.'

'Sometimes, sir,' he answered gloomily, 'I think it's a
bloody miracle she moves at all.'

We shook with a gentle ague as the engines picked up
speed, slipped down the channel of thick Mersey water,
passed the tolling buoys and the Bar light, out into the
Irish sea; in the afternoon a sharp sea-wind blew down
the deck and the Welsh mountains were huddling on the
horizon. I pranced delightedly round the ship, which was
now musical with the wind, looking at everything like a
schoolboy in the Science Museum.

I had a letter in my pocket from Wendy, which I purposely kept unopened until we were under way. It was a short prim note, wishing me a good voyage, hoping my headaches were better, and mentioning that I was not to think of ourselves as betrothed any longer. It appeared she had become enamoured of the son of the local draper. I tore the letter up and scattered it over the side: the pieces spread on the sea and were left behind. I laughed. I felt a cad, a devilish cad. But now, surely, I was allowed to be: I was a sailor. A wife in every port for me! I thought. Watch out, my girls, watch out! A rollicking sailor lad, indeed! With a snatch of sea-shanty on my lips I went below for a cup of tea, aware that I was perhaps not quite myself.

*   *   *   *

My elation lasted less than a day. The next morning I was sick.

The *Lotus* creaked and groaned her way through the water like an old lady in a bargain sale. She climbed to the top of a wave, paused for breath, shook herself, and slid helplessly into the trough of the next. I lay on my bunk and watched the sprightly horizon jumping round the porthole, trying to think about eminently terrestial objects, such as the Albert Hall.

Easter put his head round the door. In his hands he had a cup of tea and a small roseless watering-can, of the type preserved for the conveyance of tepid water in English country hotels.

'Good morning, Doctor,' he said briefly. 'Will you be in for breakfast?'

I rolled my head on the pillow.

'Not feeling too good, Doctor?'

'I think I am going to die.'

He nodded, gravely assessing the clinical findings.

'Throwing up much?' he asked pleasantly.

'Everything.'

'If I may take the liberty, a good meal is what you want. Plate of fried eggs and bacon and you'll be right as rain. Works like a charm. Hold it a moment, Doctor, I'll fetch a bowl.'

I held the bowl like a mother with a newborn infant.

'Feeling better now you've got all that up?' he asked solicitously.

'A bit.'

A thought struck him.

'Wouldn't like a bit of cold beef and a few pickles, would you? They'd do just as well.'

'No, no, no! I don't want anything. Nothing at all. I just want to be left alone.'

'Very good, Doctor. Just as you say. Perhaps you might feel like a bit of lunch?'

'I doubt it very much.'

He left me in ecstatic solitude. I lay rigidly on the bunk, concentrating on the words stencilled, by order of the Ministry of Transport, immediately above me: CERTI-FIED TO ACCOMMODATE 1 SEAMAN. Seaman, indeed! All I wanted to see was a tree.

It was essential to keep my mind fixed on something beyond the clouds of nausea spiralling round me, so I started to count the rivets in the deckhead. I had reached ninety-eight when Hornbeam came in. He was smoking a pipe.

'Hello, Doc! I hear you're off colour. What's the trouble?'

'I'm seasick.'

He looked surprised.

'Yes, I suppose she is pitching a bit,' he admitted, glancing through the porthole. 'Do you mind if I use one of your matches?'

He blew mouthfuls of smoke into the cabin.

'Better out than in,' he said, as I put the bowl down again.

'I suppose so.'

'You know what, Doc? I'm going to give you a genuine cure for seasickness. I can't often treat a doctor, but this is just the thing. Do you want to try it?'

'What is it?'

'A pint of sea-water. It's an old sailors' cure. When I was an apprentice it was the only thing that stopped me on my first voyage. If we were sick we got kicked down the bridge ladder and given a pint glass just out of the sea-bucket by the Mate. Shall I get you some?'

I raised my hand.

'I think I'd rather not have anything at all at the moment, thank you.'

'As you like, Doc. I'm only making a suggestion. Have you tried covering one eye?'

'It wasn't much good.'

'No, I don't believe it is. Damn! Can I have another match? My pipe's gone out again.'

'Would you mind lighting it outside? It's a bit—a bit strong at the moment.'

'Oh, sorry! I didn't think of that.'

I called weakly after him at the door.

'How long is this likely to go on for?'

He calculated for a few seconds.

'Not very long. I should say we'd be in pretty calm water in five or six days.'

'Five or six days!'

I groaned.

I lay and tried to analyse my condition, like the dying surgeon, John Hunter. It was, of course, a ridiculously simple malady when one looked at it with scientific detachment. The endolymph in my semi-circular canals was stimulating the endings of my cochlear nerve, which transmitted influences to the brain and initiated the reflex arc of vomiting. It should be easy for a little will-power to inhibit the reflex. After all, the brain was the master. . . . I exercised the will-power.

'Morning!' Trail said from the doorway. 'When you've got your head out of that bowl I'll tell you a sure-fire cure for seasickness.'

I fell back on the pillow. I had given up. When the angel of death arrived I would shake him cordially by the hand.

Trail came over to the bunk. He put his hands in his trouser pockets and pulled out two bottles of stout.

'Guinness,' he said proudly. 'Drink these and you'll be fine by lunch-time. Works like magic.'

'Oh God!' I said. 'Oh God, oh God!'

Trail looked puzzled.

'What's the matter? Don't you like stout? Here, take it easy! That one nearly went over my uniform.'

He left me wondering submissively how long it would be before Easter came back and started talking about lunch. And it was bound to be Irish stew.

*   *   *   *

After three days the sea and I achieved a compromise. The sun came out, the wind dropped and lost its malice, the water was tidied up like a room after a wild party. For myself, I learned to lean against the sway of the ship, and I felt well enough to risk lunch in the saloon.

It was my first meal at sea. I sat with the Captain, the Chief Engineer, Hornbeam and Archer, and the Chief Steward, a thin little mouse-faced man called Whimble. As soon as the bell rang we converged on the dining saloon with the briskness of seaside boarders: Captain Hogg disliked anyone to be late.

I was on the Captain's right hand, the Mate on his left. The Chief Engineer faced the Captain, and the other two sat themselves between.

'Ah, Doctor!' Captain Hogg said, jovially enough. 'Decided to join us at last, have you?'

'Yes, sir.'

He unfolded his napkin and tucked it under his chin with deliberation.

'Seasickness,' he said slowly, 'is entirely mental. You imagine it.'

I shrugged my shoulders.

'Well,' I said, in my professional tone, 'there are more complicated reasons than that. I admit there may be a psychological element. But there is obviously some fault with the balancing apparatus in the ears, and probably with the gastric nerves.'

The Captain broke a roll.

'No.' He said it decisively. 'It is entirely mental.'

He started drinking soup loudly.

No one spoke until he had finished.

'Mr. McDougall,' he said, slipping half a roll into his mouth, 'have you got that book you were going to lend me at supper last night?'

The Chief looked up. He was a thin, wrinkled Scot with a face dominated by a thick strip of sandy eyebrow, from which his eyes looked out like a couple of Highland gamekeepers inspecting poachers through the undergrowth.

'Aye,' he said. 'You mean *The Squeaker?*'

The Captain nodded.

'That's it. I like a bit of Peter Cheyney.'

'But surely,' I said immediately, '*The Squeaker* was by Edgar Wallace? It was written over twenty years ago.'

'No,' the Captain said. 'It was Peter Cheyney.'

'You know, sir, I'm perfectly . . .'

'Peter Cheyney,' he said, with the emphasis of a full stop. He then fell upon a plate of mutton chops, which disappeared into his mouth like a rush-hour crowd going down an escalator.

We continued eating in silence.

Captain Hogg finished his chops and brought his knife and fork together with a flourish.

'Mr. Whimble,' he said.

'Sir!'

The Chief Steward jumped, and choked over a chop bone.

'I have, I suppose, tasted worse chops than these. In a fifth-rate café on the Mexican coast possibly. Why don't you throw the cook over the side? If he'd served filth like this to the Captain when I was an apprentice the fellow would have had his bottom kicked round the deck.'

'I'm sorry, Captain,' Whimble mumbled. 'I'll see to it.'

'I should think so. You never get cooking like you used to. All they think about these days are vitamins and calories, and such stuff. What good's that to a man? Fad, that's all it is. You don't need vitamins or calories,' he said with disgust. 'Eh, Doctor?'

'Well, they are really two quite different factors. And vitamins are terribly important.'

'Bosh! I'm not a doctor—I don't pretend to be. But if you get a good bellyful of meat and spuds every day you'll be all right.'

'You must have vitamins,' I insisted, but feebly.

'Vitamins are bosh, Doctor. Bosh!'

I began to see that opinions were forbidden, even professional ones. Our mealtimes were going to be rollicking.

4

THE next morning after breakfast I went to my cabin, wedged myself on the settee, and again opened *War and Peace* at page one. I had not felt well enough to start the book since we sailed, but now I looked forward to a leisurely stroll through its pages during the rest of the voyage. I had almost reached the end of the first paragraph when a conversation started in the alleyway outside my cabin door.

The door was on a hook for ventilation, so I was able to overhear it clearly. There were two speakers, who used the adenoidal grunts with which the citizens of Liverpool communicate with each other.

'Ullo,' said one. 'Whatcher doin', la'?'

'Come to see ——-ing quack.'

'Ar. What's ——-ing trouble, la'?'

'Dunno. Reckon I must've picked up a ——-ing dose, or something.'

'Where, in Liverpeule?'

' 'Sright. Nice bit of skirt she was too.'

'You can never tell, la'.'

'——-ing right there.'

A short silence.

'What's quack like?'

'Oh, he's a young ——er.'

'Reckon he's much good?'

'——ing medical student, most likely.'

'If we was homeward bound reckon I'd wait and see a proper doctor,' the sufferer said. I opened the door. 'Good morning, Doc,' he added brightly. 'Can you see us a second, in private like?'

'Go down to the hospital,' I said coldly. 'I'll be along in a few minutes.'

'Very good, Doctor.'

When I arrived at the hospital I found that Easter had diagnosed and prescribed for the condition with an efficiency founded on wide experience of it.

'Take these, chum,' he said, handing over a bottle of sulphathiazole tablets, 'and in a couple of days you'll be feeling like a box of birds, as they say in New Zealand.'

The patient stuffed the bottle in his waistband and jauntily walked out.

'Don't you think I ought to give him a short lecture?' I suggested.

Easter seemed to find this amusing.

'We all has our thoughtless moments, Doctor, don't we? Take a card,' he said, abruptly drawing a pack from his pocket. 'Any one. Don't let me see it.'

I took one automatically.

'Right,' he said. 'I will now shuffle them, see? No deception. You could have taken any card in the pack. Let me concentrate.' He screwed up his fat face in a spasm of thought. 'Four of diamonds,' he said.

'That is perfectly correct. Though I hardly think we

should be doing this sort of thing when we are supposed to be treating patients.'

Easter slipped the cards back into the top pocket of his jacket with a subdued air of triumph.

'Dr. Flowerday always liked me to show him a few tricks. Used to have him in fits, sometimes. Didn't half get narked when he couldn't find how they was done.'

'And how was that one done, if I may ask?'

'Them's all four of diamonds, actual,' Easter said carelessly, tapping his pocket.

'You seem to be quite a specialist in this sort of thing.'

'For three years ashore I was Pin Hung, the Famous Chinese Magician. Round the halls. Mostly the North—Barrow, Carlisle, Sunderland. Grimsby was my favourite. Always hit the jackpot in Grimsby. I've a book of cuttings down below. . . .'

'All right. Later on in the voyage, possibly.'

He flicked three cards from his sleeve and manipulated them on the top of a tin of bandages.

'Now then, Doctor. Try your luck. Bet you a dollar that you can't spot the lady.'

'Easter,' I said with interest, 'how is it that you have come to land up in your present position? A man of your peculiar talents would be far more at home on the race-course than in a ship's hospital.'

'That's the trouble, Doctor. I worked the race trains for years. But I got fed up with it. You can get put inside too many times.'

I stared at him.

'Do you mean—are you trying to say that you have been in prison?'

I was alarmed. In shore practice this was not a condition usually found in one's colleagues.

'Ho, yes,' he replied, with the air of a man admitting he knew Brighton or Scarborough fairly well. 'Didn't like it much, though. Too bloody cold in winter.'

'So you came to sea instead?'

'That's right, Doctor. Used to be on the Western Ocean run for donkeys' years in the big passenger boats. When I was a lad that is, and could run about a bit more. So I came back to it. Signed on as a steward. It's a good life, and you gets your grub regular. I took this job on when a mate of mine jumped ship in Sydney and I helped out in the surgery homeward bound. I like it better than waiting in the saloon. More dignified. And Dr. Flowerday used to let me dispose of surplus equipment and stores on the coast, if I could. Penicillin and such like, that ain't got long to go before it's U.S. That be all right with you, Doctor? Dr. Flowerday and I used to have an understanding about the proceeds.'

'I think we shall have to consider that later.'

'Very good, Doctor. There's one of the crew sick in his cabin.'

'Then why the devil didn't you tell me before? Instead of fooling around with all these damn card tricks.'

'There ain't no hurry, Doctor. It's only Chippy. The Carpenter.'

'What's the matter with him?'

'He's having one of his turns.'

I was suspicious. A diagnosis of the turns, to which over half of the middle-aged population of the country seems liable, can represent any condition from attacks of flatulence to full-blown epileptic fits.

'We'd better go and see him at once.'

'Very good, Doctor.'

I followed Easter aft, to the crew's accommodation in the poop. We went up an iron ladder to a door with CARPENTER AND LAMPTRIMMER stencilled over it. It was a bleak little cabin, with green-painted steel bulkheads and a couple of metal bunks one above the other. The only decoration was a photograph of an oblong tombstone with 'Mother's Grave' written underneath it.

On the top bunk was the patient, huddled under a grey ship's blanket. I gave him a shake. A head poked out at me, and I recognized the man with the lamp I had met at the top of the gangway. He needed a shave, there was dried saliva at the corners of his mouth, and his eyes looked like a couple of cherries on a blancmange.

'Aghurrr!' he said.

'Now what's the trouble, my man?' I started briskly.

He disregarded me. His eyes were on something else in the cabin, behind me. He pointed shakily to the corner.

'Get away you bastards!' he yelled.

I jumped.

'Now don't get excited . . .' I said nervously.

He crouched into a corner of the bunk, pulling the blanket tightly round him.

'Get away!' he screamed. 'Get away from me!'

He brushed something from the bunk rail.

'What is it?' I asked. 'What's the trouble?'

The man started muttering, so that I had to lean closely over him to hear.

'It's them dogs,' he said. 'Bloody great Alsatians. Bloody great green ones. Look! Five of the bastards!'

I turned sharply round to Easter.

'This man has got D.T.s,' I announced.

'Ho, yes,' Easter said casually, not shifting from the

doorway. 'Been having them for years. Long as I can remember, anyway.'

'But we must do something about it! I hope you realize this is a serious condition? You seem to treat it very lightly.'

'He always gets 'em about this part of the trip. He'll be as right as rain for weeks now. Been on the booze since we sailed. Says it makes him sad leaving Liverpool.'

The patient rattled the bunk.

'Get your paws orf of my face!' he yelled.

'If I might make so bold, Doctor,' Easter said, still leaning on the door, 'I would say this was an occasion for the medical comforts.'

'Medical comforts? What on earth are you talking about?'

'Bottle of brandy,' he explained. 'It's issued buckshee, like, for the hospital. You can get another from the Chief Steward if you indent for it.'

'But I haven't seen anything of this brandy.'

'I usually keeps it in my cabin, Doctor. Dr. Flowerday and I had an understanding about it.'

'Is there any left?'

'Almost half, Doctor,' he said proudly. 'Dr. Flowerday used to give him a glassful and talk to him, gentle like, as if he was a baby. Worked like a charm. Shall I fetch the bottle?'

'Here they come again!' the patient shouted.

'Perhaps you'd better,' I said.

I gave him a tumbler of brandy and explained that the five green Alsatians were not really present, like a nurse soothing a night-scared child. After a couple of glasses and half an hour's persuasion I had reduced the intruders to three in number, and to terriers of normal colour. I felt entitled to be satisfied with this. I left the patient sleeping in his bunk with the empty glass in his hand and went back to my cabin.

'Seen many cases like him ashore?' Easter asked with interest, collecting the remains of the brandy.

'No. I have not. There seems a great difference, Easter, between the practice of medicine on shore and at sea.'

'Funny you should say that. Same thing always struck me about the doctors.'

5

IT is remarkable what spiritual contentment can be obtained from washing your own socks. I soaped a pair in the basin and hung them to dry on a line Easter had stretched across my cabin. I glowed with a modest sense of achievement. This was the first time I had been obliged to do any washing, which I had previously looked upon as an esoteric feminine function comparable with giving birth.

The crew of the *Lotus* did their own laundering—even Captain Hogg, who appeared in the early afternoon on the strip of deck round his cabin with a bundle of white uniforms under his arm and a basket of clothes-pegs. The other officers hung their shirts over their bunks and smartened them afterwards in the bathroom with the Third Mate's travelling iron. Down aft, the crew set aside Sunday afternoon for the laundry, when it was usual to see large firemen and deckhands dressed only in underpants and tattoos scrubbing their singlets with bar soap in the fire-buckets. The clothes were then strung thickly round the winches and ventilators and flapped round the stern of the ship like some fantastic signal.

Drying was simple, for we had reached the Tropics and the ship's company was in white uniforms. I had only to fix a white cover on my Company's regulation cap, but the officers appeared unexpectedly one morning in white shorts and shirts, like a crop of snowdrops. The other hands were less affected by the order. Easter changed his blue serge jacket for a white one, but the rest were permitted the informality of uniform usual in the Merchant Service and did no more than roll their dungaree trousers half-way up their calves and remove their shirts.

'We should have been in whites two days ago,' Hornbeam grumbled. 'It's the Old Man's fault.'

'Why? What's he done now?'

'The old bastard sunbathes every afternoon and keeps us in blues until his knees are brown.'

I felt I was becoming quite a sailor. I let my days pass uncaringly, carried away in the drift of the sea routine. In a ship everybody seems constantly to be getting up or going to bed. The watch changes every fourth hour, which brings one of the mates, warm from his bunk, to the bridge, and sends a couple of engineers scuttling down the complicated ladders into the engine-room and stokehold. As well as the officers, two A.B.s go on the bridge to take turns at the wheel, and a gang of greasers and firemen troop below. All this movement is set off by the ship's bell on the bridge, which rings through each watch an arithmetical progression of half-hourly strokes.

Members of the ship's company who had no watches to keep—people like Whimble, Easter, and myself—all arranged their days round the after-dinner siesta. In the afternoon the whole ship died. All hands, apart from those essential for the running of the vessel, tottered away from the saloon table and, encouraged by a weighty meal and the noon session of gin, crashed gratefully into their bunks. This was a habit I found condemnable, but irresistible. In medical school and practice the afternoon had been my busiest time, and I was determined to pass the hours between one and four studying *War and Peace*. At first I never drank before the meal and avoided the cook's suet roll, of which Captain Hogg must have eaten several fathoms every voyage. But—whether I was the subject of mass-suggestion or sea air contains some subtle narcotic— I was unconscious before I got the taste of the ship's cheese out of my mouth, and I stayed asleep until Easter shook me at four with a cup of tea and a small piece of confectionery known in the Merchant Service as a tab-nab. This habit I regarded nervously as the first indication of moral degeneration.

At five-thirty every evening my bath was run by Boswell, the bath steward. Boswell, like Easter, had seen better days, and the courtly manners he had learned in big P. & O.s and Cunarders had not deserted him. Whatever the temperature, he wore a shining white jacket, a stiff wing collar, and a black bow tie. He would arrive at my cabin door at half-past five precisely, a clean blue-and-white towel folded over his arm, and announce 'Your bath awaits, Doctor,' as if it were an important delegation. He followed me to the officers' bathroom, which smelled like a seaside cave at low tide, spread the towel over the chair, and mixed the water with his skinny hand. He dipped in a foot-long thermometer with a little metal bucket at the end, anxiously inspected the tempera-ture, and made a careful adjustment to the taps (later I found the thermometer had not worked for several years). He then poured some fresh hot water from a large shining copper can into a small bowl for the feet, and laid on the white wooden rack across the bath my flannel, a long-handled scrubbing brush, a loofah, and a bar of sea-water soap.

'Would there be anything else you require, sir?' he asked every evening. I found it difficult to complicate such a simple act as taking a bath any further, and he would bow deeply and retire backwards through the steam. I knew he did so with disappointment, for a bath suggested to him as many variations as soup to a French chef. Every few days he would press me to take a few spoonfuls of mustard in it, or some washing soda, or a tumbler of rose-water. 'Might I recommend a little Sloane's?' he asked once. 'I used to put it in regularly for one doctor I looked after in the Cunard. Very good for the joints, I believe.'

Boswell's manners were unfortunately not sufficient to overcome the discomforts of the *Lotus's* bathroom. There were no portholes or ventilators, so water collected on the deckhead as efficiently as in the main condenser in the engine-room, and thence fell thickly in rusty brown drops. The deck was covered with some crumbling material that left potholes to trip the bather and make him catch his head or his shins against sharp projecting pieces of steel. The bath itself was shaped like a coffin, and was furnished with a pair of fearsome taps that gave between them hot and cold sea water and a disproportionate amount of steam. There was an alternative—the fresh-water shower outside Hornbeam's cabin, but owing to some subtle mechanical fault many feet below in the engine-room this emitted only ice-cold water or superheated steam, and after escaping a third-degree burn I decided to stick to the safer tepid waters under Boswell's supervision.

Boswell did not stop at baths: far greater was his pride

in the officers' lavatories. These were not much more efficient than the bath, and in rough weather became alarmingly unreliable. But to Boswell they were a porcelain monument to his own calling. He spent the morning cleaning and polishing them, and on our arrival for inspection would bow low and flush each as we passed with the jaunty pride of the satisfied artist.

'There's more in lavatories than meets the eye, sir,' he explained to me one day, with a sigh. 'You've got to *understand* lavatories to do this job.' I gathered from Easter that as he contentedly did his morning task Boswell dreamed of his retirement in charge of a small underground nest of them at one of the quieter corners of Liverpool.

My professional duties were not exacting. I saw a couple of patients in the morning, perhaps half a dozen at five. The most common trouble was the constipation, doctor. This I first treated with pharmacopœial doses of the usual remedies, but I soon found it was necessary to multiply the amount by three for most of the patients and by five for the Bos'n and firemen. There were boils and warts, a few burns from the engine-room, and several vague illnesses whose leading symptom was a disinclination to work. We had a few more cases resulting from careless choice of friends during our last nights in Liverpool. The approach to the medical attendant by sufferers from this embarrassing condition varied from the shifty request— with a sidelong glance at Easter—to ' 'Ave a word wiv you a minute, Doctor,' to the full-blooded storming of the surgery by the experienced invalid with his 'Say, Doc, can you fix this for us by Friday?'

At eleven we inspected the ship. Hornbeam, Whimble, McDougall, and myself gathered outside the saloon door and saluted when Captain Hogg's boots appeared on the companionway from his cabin. This homage he returned with the grace of a publican handing back a counterfeit half-crown.

We lined up behind him and set off touring the decks, each of us trying to look as disagreeable as possible. We filed in and out of Boswell's lavatories with dignity, and zealously searched for dust under the coconut matting. The progress was broken only when Captain Hogg's eye was jarred by something that gave him displeasure, when he would turn his fury not only on the man responsible but on his parents as well. At first I shivered at the onslaught: then I grew to appreciate the range and power of the Captain's imagination and the felicity with which he turned his sentences, until I listened to him with fascination. As for the victims, they shrugged their shoulders and took no notice. Raving Captains were just like storms at sea: you had to put up with them until they blew themselves out, and not become unreasonably excited.

After inspection the Captain went on the bridge to supervise the daily ceremony of finding the noon position of the ship. I went up there only once, because Captain Hogg looked on visitors like a sour landowner spotting picnickers on his front lawn. It was a shady, restful place, lined with dark wood and brass, like an old-fashioned saloon bar. The sea was surprisingly far below, and the only sound was the irregular loud clicking of the gyro repeater, like the ticking of an arrythmic clock. Abaft the bridge was the chartroom, where rulers, set-squares, and neatly sharpened pencils were arranged like a tidy school desk, and the chronometers nestled under thick glass like a pair of premature infants in an incubator. Hornbeam once offered me his sextant and let me work out our position, but I disgusted him by putting the *Lotus* within a few miles of Cleveland, Ohio.

I spent most of my time chatting to the officers off watch, leaning on the rail, playing quoits, or nosing round the deck. I was beginning to learn what everything was called. Ships have a distinct anatomy of their own, and our daily rounds were as confusing to me as my first demonstrations in the dissecting room. I recognized fairly early on the difference between port and starboard, fore and aft, and a binnacle and a barnacle; but I was still uncertain where to find such obscure pieces of marine furnishing as the jumper stays, the monkey island, and the shrouds.

*   *   *   *

The tenth morning of the voyage I sat down resolutely in my cabin and took *War and Peace* from the locker. Somehow I had not yet found time to pass the first page. I opened it, smoothed down the paper, and began again the first paragraph. Hornbeam rattled the jalousie door and came in.

'Morning, Doc! Everything bearing an even strain?'

'Good morning, Chief,' I said. 'I think so, thanks very much.'

'Good.'

Picking up the first volume of *War and Peace* he neatly squashed a cockroach that was scuttling across the bulkhead.

'These damn roaches,' he said. 'Come out in families once it turns hot. Had any in bed with you?'

'No, not yet.'

He pulled a tobacco tin from his pocket.

'Would you like the makings?' he asked, offering it.

'No, thank you. I'm afraid it's a nautical knack I haven't picked up.'

'It's easy enough. Can't stand tailor-mades.'

He neatly rolled a cigarette between his fingers and thumbs. Whenever I tried the same manœuvre I squeezed the tobacco out like the cream from an éclair.

'Wish you'd have a look at the Sparks, Doc,' Hornbeam continued affably.

'Why, what's the trouble?'

'I just saw him shake hands with a lifeboat.'

'Ah, yes. I was rather afraid something like that might happen.'

Our Wireless Operator was probably the luckiest man on the ship. He was one of those blithe people who live in a world of their own. He had been at sea for forty years, crouched over a telegraph key with the staccato song of Morse in his ears. This seemed to have induced psychological changes in him. For the rest of us, our universe was bounded by the steel and wooden limits of the *Lotus*—but not the Sparks. He passed his day in the company of soft-skinned maidens and amiable philosophers, with whom he could often be seen laughing, conversing, and singing while he walked round the deck or sat in the corner of his cabin. Sometimes he did a coy little dance with some of his companions, or played a simple game; and occasionally they would have a restrained tiff, which always ended happily in the way just observed by the Mate. The Sparks was by far the happiest person under Captain Hogg's command.

'I suppose he's quite harmless?' I asked. 'I mean, he doesn't send out dangerous messages or anything?'

'Oh, he's not in that stage yet,' Hornbeam assured me tolerantly. 'I've seen a good many worse than him. The

Morse gets 'em in the end. I just thought you ought to know. I saw him kissing a ventilator yesterday,' he added darkly.

'We are all entitled to our little aberrations, I suppose.'

'You're right there, Doc. Life at sea wouldn't be possible without a bit of give and take. Old Sparks is all right. Just a bit dippy. Like some of these tanker types.'

'Tanker types?'

He nodded, lighting the cigarette and filling the cabin with smoke.

'Men in tankers. It's a dog's life. They run to places like the Persian Gulf and they can unload in a couple of days. That means the boys don't get much of a run ashore when they're home. Besides, you can't live on top of a few thousand tons of petrol all your life without getting a bit queer. Of course, they get the money. . . . But is it worth it? Friend of mine went mate in a tanker to make a bit and ended up by cutting his throat. Made a hell of a mess in the chartroom, so they told me.'

From Hornbeam's conversation I gathered that suicide at sea had a panache not seen ashore.

'I think I'll stick to dry cargo,' I said. 'That seems dangerous enough for doctors.'

'Are you coming to the Third's do to-night?' Hornbeam asked. 'That's the reason I looked in.'

'I didn't know he was having one.'

'It's his birthday—twenty-first—and he's having a few beers. You're invited.'

'I don't drink much, you know.'

'Oh, don't be scared, Doc. None of us drinks while we're at sea. I'll say you're coming.'

The party was after supper, in the Third Mate's cabin.

As I was anxious not to appear at all anti-social I was the first to arrive.

1 had not been in his cabin before. It was smaller than mine, with just enough room for a man to stand between the bunk and the strip of settee on the opposite bulkhead. There was a porthole over the settee and a forced-draught vent in the deckhead that stabbed a narrow stream of cold air across the bunk. Opposite the door was a small desk covered completely with bottles of gin. The rest of the cabin was covered with girls.

They were everywhere—in frames over the bunk, pasted to the bulkhead, suspended from the pipes crossing the deckhead. There were plain photographs of ordinary girls, shadowy nudes from *Men Only*, taut scissor-legged girls in impossible brassières from *Esquire*, a few bright beer advertisements from Australia of surprised but un-resisting girls with their skirts caught in mangles, car doors, stiles, and dog leads, girls with no clothes playing on the beach, girls with all their clothes caught in a highly selective gale, even pictures of Chinese girls covered from neck to ankle.

'Come in, Doc!' the Third said. 'Have a peg.'

He pushed a glass into my hand and half-filled it with gin in one motion.

'Happy birthday,' I said faintly. 'You seem to have an eye for art.'

'Got to brighten the old cart up a bit. Here's to you.'

He pointed above the bunk to the photograph of a sharp-chinned young lady trying earnestly to look like Dorothy Lamour.

'That's a nice bit of crumpet. Met her in Hull last voyage. She's an intelligent bit, mind you,' he added seriously. 'Works in Boots' library.'

He indicated her rival next to her.

'Now there's a girl for you. Came across her in Adelaide. Last time we were there her brother came and socked me on the nose. She still writes to me, though.'

'I hope he didn't hurt you.'

'He did a bit. He's one of the wharfies. That one's from St. John. But this Sheila here's the best of the bunch. Lives in Durban. Father's got pots of cash.'

'You seem to scatter your affections pretty widely.'

'They all love sailors. When a girl knows a fellow's going half-way round the world in a week's time she takes the brakes off a bit. Have a seat on the bunk.'

I saw down and rested my head uncomfortably on the paper bosom of a blonde.

The other guests arrived together. There was Hornbeam, the crazy Sparks, Whimble, the Second Steward, and the Chief, Second, Third, and Fourth Engineers. Archer was absent, keeping Hornbeam's watch on the bridge. The ten of us crammed ourselves into the tiny cabin. Hornbeam had his elbow in my face and his shoes on the Chief Engineer's knees. Whimble wedged himself behind the door and stuck his feet against the end of the bunk. The host struggled between everyone's legs, handing out drinks. I felt that something would shortly give way and project the lot of us into the sea.

The Third's health was drunk by all hands.

'Have another, Doc,' he said.

'No, really . . .'

'Come off it! It's only five bob a bottle.' He half-filled my tumbler again. 'How do you like the sea?' he asked.

'It is a very interesting form of existence.'

'Of course, you realize this is only part of it,' Hornbeam

explained. 'It varies a good bit. As you know, British ships are in three classes.'

'Tankers . . .?'

'No. First of all there's the P. & O. Then there's the Merchant Navy, which is the set-up we're in. After that there's the Old Grey Funnel line.'

'Also known as the Royal Navy,' McDougall explained. 'It was nationalized years ago.'

'The P. & O. must not be confused with ordinary hookers,' Hornbeam continued. 'It's a sort of—well, a floating Horse Guards, if you get me. They hate to be called Merchantmen. If you make a noise drinking your soup . . .'

'They wear swords and spurs,' Trail said.

'I don't believe it.'

'Well, they ought to. Oh, very posh, very posh. Good shower of bastards on the whole, though. Have some more gin.'

'Not for . . . Oh, all right, as you've poured it out. It tastes better than the stuff you get ashore.'

'Everything does. By the way, you know the Second Engineer, Doc? Mr. Macpherson.'

'Pleased to meet you.'

'Mr. MacPhail the Third and Mr. Macintosh the Fourth.'

'What, are you all Scots in the engine-room?'

'We've a Taffy and a couple of Geordies,' Macpherson said. 'Had to have them in to do the dirty work.'

'You know what they say,' McDougall added proudly. 'If you open the engine-room hatch of any British ship and shout "Jock" someone'll be bound to come up.'

McPhail started singing 'I belong to Glasgow,' but petered out for lack of support.

'Coming ashore with us in Santos, Doc?' Hornbeam asked.

'Certainly. I intend to take advantage of the voyage to broaden my education.'

'Santos will broaden it all right. Plenty of nice girls there.'

'I'm sure I should be pleased if you'd introduce me to them.'

This remark started everyone laughing.

'You don't need any introductions. It's keeping them away that's the trouble.'

'Well, I shall not be interested in meeting any of that sort.'

'Oh, you'll have to come with us to Madame Mimi's,' Hornbeam said reproachfully. 'It would be like going to London and missing the Houses of Parliament.'

'Are you suggesting,' I said coldly, 'that I should visit a brothel?'

'Where the hell else do you think there is to go in Santos?' Trail said testily. 'Anyway, Madame Mimi's is as respectable as the Liverpool Museum.'

'I wouldn't put that past suspicion,' Hornbeam said.

Trail cut the conversation short by pouring out gin all round and beginning a complicated story about two sailors losing their way in Lime Street station.

After an hour everyone was pretty cheerful.

'Don't make such a row,' Trail said. 'Father'll hear.'

'To hell with Father,' I heard myself say.

'Spoken like a sailor, Doc!' Hornbeam slapped me on the chest. 'Good old Doc! Best one I've ever sailed with.'

'I say, really . . .'

'You're the only one that's sane!'

This brought a round of applause.

c

'You're all mad at sea,' I said defiantly. 'The lot of you.'

The company immediately indicated their disbelief with the usual word.

'You are,' I said. 'Or you wouldn't be here.'

'Have some more gin,' Trail said.

'Thank you.' I swallowed another mouthful. 'As I was saying. I have made a diagnosis. From careful—not to say exacting—study of you in the past ten days I conclude that you're all suffering from the death wish.'

'What the hell's that?' McDougall asked angrily.

I held up a hand.

'Silence. As a disciple of Hippocrates I demand respect and silence. The death wish. When you are born all you want to do is die.'

This again filled the cabin with derision.

'Shut up, you blokes. Let the poor blighter speak,' Trail said.

I continued. 'That is what the psychologists say. Some people hang themselves. Others go into monasteries and . . . and things. Some climb mountains and live in caves. Others write poetry. Look at English poetry,' I demanded hotly of Hornbeam. 'Look at it! Redolent with the death wish!' I screwed up my eyes and struck an attitude of recitation.

'. . . *for many a time*
I have been half in love with easeful Death,'
I declaimed stumblingly.

'*Call'd him soft names in many a musèd rhyme,*
To take into the air my quiet . . .'

I slipped off the bunk, but Hornbeam caught me.

'Death wish to the eyebrows, the lot of you! You withdraw—to sea. To sea! That's what it is!'

'You're full of prune-juice, Doc,' someone said.

'I will not have insults,' I cried. 'If you would care to defend yourself like a gentleman, I shall take you up on it. You have the death wish, by God! You've all got it. So had Nelson. I've got it as well.'

I fell over McDougall's feet and no one bothered to pick me up.

6

THE next morning I was suffering from a sharp attack of the death wish. But my performance had raised me surprisingly in the eyes of my shipmates. My earnest years as a medical student, my dignified excursion into practice, my prim approach to seafaring had built a scaffold underneath me: the Third Mate's gin had slipped the bolt.

My companions were relieved to find that I was not only sane but human: for my part, I began to realize that the sea, which washes away terrestrial affectations and inhibitions, had a great deal to recommend it. Sailors are of the few remaining people who make their way in companies across the unsignposted face of the world with the help of the sun and the stars, and spend most of their lives lying at the unhindered fancy of the weather. Their sense of values in human and elemental behaviour is therefore unblunted; they look on their existence as a long uproarious joke relieved by not unentertaining interludes of necessary tragedy. I thought them the last of the Elizabethans.

I believe there is no process so restful as moving at

bicycle pace through the sunshine of the South Atlantic. We were steaming at ten knots, which meant we should be about three weeks reaching Santos. The metallic fragment of England in which we all existed—except the Wireless Operator—creaked easily onwards with a faint haze of smoke rolling from the funnel, scattering the nimble flying fish with her bow. Even crossing the Line caused no more disturbance than my having to stand drinks all round. The hot sun welded the days together so that they became indistinguishable. It was impossible to tell whether it was Tuesday or Thursday, and it didn't matter.

Only twice a week were we reminded of the calendar— Friday and Sunday. At four-thirty on Friday afternoons we had boat drill. Captain Hogg stood on the bridge and pulled the cord of the whistle, which sent us scurrying up the ladders in our blue-and-orange life-jackets to the boat-deck. I was in boat number four, in charge of the Third Mate, who ticked our names off with a roll-call. I was alarmed to find that among my companions in an emergency would be the Carpenter with a tendency to D.T.s and a pleasant-faced greaser who, I heard from Easter, had just returned from a ten-year stretch for armed robbery.

'Swing out!' Captain Hogg shouted through the loud hailer.

The canvas covers were stripped off the boats, and three men set to the handle of each davit to lean it out from the ship's side. When this had been done to Captain Hogg's satisfaction the boats were swung in again and everyone dispersed.

'Board of Trade sports,' Trail said with disgust. 'Waste of time.'

'Why do we do it then?' I asked.

'Oh, it has to go in the log-book. There'd be hell in Liverpool if we didn't. Some skippers cook the log, but not this baby. Anything to give him a chance of bawling through a loud hailer.'

Sunday was recognizable, as it was the only occasion when we flew the flag at sea. From eight to midday the red ensign waved from the gaff on the mainmast, to convince the Almighty that we had not forgotten him— for there was no one else but ourselves to see it. The appearance of the flag that symbolized the Sabbath was greeted warmly by all hands, not through reverence but because, under Ministry of Transport regulations, we all got an extra half-day's pay.

Sunday was also marked by the ceremony of full inspection. This was ordered by Captain Hogg's copy of *Instructions for Masters*, the manual through which the Fathom Steamship Company directed and advised their commanders, which contained in its yellow pages regulations designed to right such nautical disasters as mutiny, epidemics of smallpox, lost anchor, and imminent shipwreck. At eleven o'clock the four of us fell in behind the Captain, who indicated the exceptional occasion by carrying a torch and a walking-stick. On the poop the ship's company was lined up ready for us—deckhands under the charge of the Bos'n on the port side, firemen and greasers to starboard, and catering staff, in fresh white jackets, standing nervously athwartships. Captain Hogg passed down the ranks scowling into each face like a vengeful but short-sighted victim at an identification parade, then we marched in and out of the little, green-painted crews' cabins that each smelt of feet and hair-oil. They had been cleaned and tidied so that nothing in the slightest degree disturbing could fall into the Captain's visual fields. The decks were scrubbed, the blankets folded ostentatiously, and the owners' possessions—varying from a guitar to a caged canary—were set in unnaturally tidy piles. Captain Hogg shone his torch beneath the bunks, inspected the undersurfaces of tables and chairs, and thrust the crook of his walking-stick into every inviting orifice. Usually his rummaging produced nothing more than a cloud of dust and an empty beer-tin, but occasionally he would drag out a saloon plate, a silver coffee-pot, a mildewed loaf, a pair of underpants, or the crumpled photograph of an inconstant girl friend.

'Mr. Hornbeam!' he would shout, waving the find under the Mate's nose. 'What's the meaning of this? Eh? We'll find the chronometers in here next!'

The last call was my hospital. Sunday was the only occasion when it was inspected, and Easter spent the morning polishing the brasswork and tipping all the small movable objects and surgical debris into a large white bin labelled 'Sterile Dressings.' As we arrived he stood smartly to attention beside the door, hiding a large black patch on the bulkhead.

'All correct, Doctor?' the Captain growled every Sunday.

'Yes, sir. All correct.'

He fixed Easter with his eye.

'Any complaints?'

'I am very happy, Captain,' Easter replied unctuously.

'All right. Pipe down, Bos'n.'

The crew were scattered to their Sunday indolence and we went up to the Captain's cabin, where we stood in a line in front of him, our caps under our arms, and he emphasized the points that had incurred his disapproval. Then we all sat down and had a gin.

There were no religious observances on board the *Lotus*—an omission that was deplored only by Easter. This surprised me. 'I didn't know you were a churchgoer,' I told him.

'Ho, yes, Doctor. I likes a nice service of a Sunday. Breaks the monotony a bit. Not much good in an old tub like this, but in the big passenger boats I used to sing hymns at the back. I've got a bit of a voice,' he added modestly.

'I'm very pleased to hear it.'

'Used to take the plate round as well. Real nice job that is. Must be the sea air what makes them generous. You see them old skinflints what wouldn't give a tanner to a blind baby at home sticking in quids and suchlike. Made quite a bit out of that in my time.'

'You mean you actually helped yourself from the collection?'

'Sort of commission, as you might say,' he explained amiably. 'Nothing much, mind you. No one knows what there is in the kitty, but you've got to be pretty nifty slipping it out before the Purser spots you. Charity begins at home, don't it, Doctor?'

*　　*　　*　　*

My clinical practice continued its easy routine, and was centred round preservation of the health of the Captain's stomach. I had never known an organ to produce such widespread clinical effects. If it functioned painlessly life was tolerable, even at mealtimes; but the first twinges of dyspepsia immediately communicated themselves to everyone on board. Fortunately I was able to denature my mixture of its explosive properties, and it

combated spiritually with the Captain's diet. My morning
visit to him with the sick-list gave me an opportunity to see
how the battle was going by judging the state of the old
gentleman's temper—a matter of importance on the ship
beyond the belief of any landsman. If he was in a good
mood he took the chit without question, and sometimes
even demonstrated extreme geniality by offering me a gin
(he saw nothing unusual in drinking after breakfast). If
my mixture was not up to strength, or if he had eaten too
many platefuls of Madras curry the night before, he
would seize the paper and scowl at it like a Tudor
monarch affirming a list of executions.

'What's wrong with that man?' he would demand,
stabbing the sheet with his blunt finger. 'McKlusky, J.,
Ordinary Seaman. Why's he off duty? What's this—
P.U.O.?'

'Pyrexia of unknown origin, sir,' I explained timidly.
'He had a temperature.'

'Well, why has he?'

'I'm afraid I don't know, sir.'

'Why don't you? You're the Doctor, aren't you? What
the devil do you think would happen to us all if I didn't
know a lighthouse when I saw one? Eh? What have you
got to say to that?'

He slammed the paper down on his desk. I said nothing
to it.

'Now, look here, Doctor,' he went on. 'I'm not in your
line, and I don't pretend to be. But I can tell you what's
wrong with this man—he's constipated. I haven't been to
sea for forty years for nothing. Give the bastard a double
dose of black draught and kick him back on duty. If he
still shirks I'll put him in the log-book. That's an order!'

'Yes, sir.'

This put me in a state of professional agitation. But Captain Hogg would have agitated the whole General Medical Council.

The Captain was at his most terrifying when conducting the ceremony of placing an offender's name in the log-book. This was the only disciplinary action left in his hands: flogging at the mainmast, keel-hauling, and hanging from the yardarm at sunset have been abolished by Parliament, and Captain Hogg made it plain that he thought the world all the worse for it.

One night shortly after we reached the Tropics I was pulled from my bunk by Hornbeam to see a couple of firemen who had been fighting in the foc's'le. Both of them were drunk. They were in the hospital, blood-spattered and muttering surly threats at each other, separated by Easter with the heavy pestle from the drug locker.

'Now keep quiet for the doctor,' he said cheerfully, 'or I'll bash your ruddy brains in with this. These two have filled each other in something proper,' he added to me as a clinical explanation.

During the two hours needed to sew them up I gathered that the pair of them, Kelly and Crosby, came from the opposite sides of a Liverpool street; and a feud had smouldered between them since they first threw stones at each other from the shelter of their mother's skirts. Too late they had found themselves both aboard the *Lotus*, and had been living in grudging amicability since we sailed. But that evening Kelly had been unable to repress any longer his opinion that Crosby's mother was not only a harlot, but the oldest and most ugly in all Liverpool, and Crosby cracked the end of a bottle and went for him.

The next morning at ten I was summoned to the

Captain's cabin, which had the ceremonially grim air
of a Portsmouth court-martial. Sitting at the desk was
Captain Hogg, an expression on his face of uninhibited
malevolence. Set before him were his gold-braided cap,
Instructions for Masters, the log-book open at the correct
page, a sheet of yellow blotting-paper, and a large silver
ink-pot with a pen in it, so that everything was at hand for
making the damning entry. Hornbeam was in a chair
beside the Captain, looking seriously at his own feet. The
Bos'n and the Donkeyman were positioned on each side of
the door, and I was ordered curtly to the corner. In the
middle of the circle were the two delinquents, twisting their
caps in their hands and throwing nervous glances round
the cabin from the gaps in their bandages.

'Right,' Captain Hogg began briskly. 'Now we are all
assembled we can begin. First of all I want to make
something perfectly plain to you two. You are going to get
a completely fair hearing this morning. Understand? You
are quite at liberty to put questions to me or any other of
the officers. You may call any witness you like in your
defence. As far as I'm concerned a man is innocent until
he's proved guilty, whether it's murder or pinching a
ha'penny stamp. You'll never find me giving a man a bad
character till it's proved. I'm a fair captain, I am. Get me?'

The two firemen nodded hesitantly.

'Very well. Now, tell me your version of the affair.'

He folded his arms judicially.

The feud that had burned so brightly a few hours
before was now outshone by the peril that faced the two
opponents. They had composed a story during breakfast, which was begun by Kelly in the tone of bitter
repentance that had occasionally swayed sympathetic
members of a magistrate's bench.

'Well, sir, it was like this 'ere, sir. Me and me mate was 'avin' a cupper tea . . .'

'You bloody liar!' Captain Hogg shouted. 'You were rotten drunk, both of you bastards! Oh yes, you were! Don't answer me back or I'll kick you round the deck. You were drunk in the foc's'le and you started fighting like the pair of goddam cut-throats you are. My God, you're a crowd of loafers up forrard! You oughtn't to be at sea, you ought to be in jail, the lot of you! Stand up straight when I'm talking to you, blast you!' He thrust a finger under Kelly's nose. 'You turn my ship into a Liverpool rough-house and you come up here with some cock-and-bull story you think I'm going to swallow. What do you take me for, eh? I was at sea when you were playing marbles in the filth of a Liverpool gutter. Mr. Hornbeam!'

'Sir?'

'You found these men fighting?'

Hornbeam nodded.

'Doctor!'

'Sir?'

'Did you or did you not find these men were drunk?'

'Well, sir, the scientific tests . . .'

'There you are! The Doctor agrees with me! You were soused, the pair of you!' He banged the desk with his fist, making the pen leap out of the ink-pot. 'Do you know what I'd like to do to you?' he demanded. 'I'd like to give you every holystone on board and make you scrub the boatdeck till the plates showed through. Then I'd put you in irons in the chain-locker and keep you on bread and water till we got back to Liverpool. That's the sort of treatment scum like you need! I'd like to put you in an open boat here and now, and get rid of the pair of you for good. Do you understand, you couple of lazy sons of bitches?'

But fortunately the Captain's justice was obligatorily tempered with mercy. 'Fined five shillings,' he muttered. 'Good morning.'

It was fortunate that Captain Hogg was, through reason of his being a captain, confined most of the day to his own quarters. He passed his time sitting in an armchair reading magazines similar to the one hiding his face on the first occasion I met him. In the corner of his cabin was a pile three feet high of these periodicals, from all parts of the English-speaking world. He consumed them earnestly and steadily, like a man with plenty of time looking up a train in Bradshaw. 'There's one thing I do like,' he announced at dinner one day, a forkful of beef and vegetables at his mouth, 'and that's a good book.'

For the rest of the voyage I bowed to his opinions like a Victorian schoolboy and took the greatest pains possible to avoid him.

The Leader of the Opposition in the *Lotus* was the Chief Engineer, McDougall. He alone of the engineers had unresented entry into the saloon and our company: the mates looked upon them instinctively as intruders, a relic of the days when thin funnels first poked their way through the proud canvas. The engineers lived away from the rest of us in tiny hot cabins clustered amidships, and ate in a pokey messroom ventilated by the oily breath of the engines. We saw them only when they leant over the rail in their black and sweaty boiler suits, or lay on their backs dissembling one of the pieces of ugly machinery that sprung from *Lotus's* deck.

McDougall had a noisy cabin by the engine-room

hatchway, in which he received visitors with a half-tumbler of neat whisky (he maintained that gin was a drink fit only for harlots). His surroundings were as untidy as a nursery. Scraps of steel and paint-pots littered the deck, the bunk sagged under pieces of dismantled machinery, and the bulkheads supported charts, graphs, a row of sombre engineering books, and an incongruous nude leaving her bath on a boilermakers' calendar. Scattered everywhere, like thistledown blown by a breeze, were scraps of half-used cotton waste.

'Where would ye all be without my engines?' he demanded. 'Do ye know what you've got to thank us for? Everything from the propeller revolutions to your shaving water and the ice in your gin.'

He thought of his engines, as Boswell did of his lavatories, as living beings possessed of souls.

'Ye'll be no damn good as an engineer till you make friends with your engines,' he told me. 'Talk to 'em, that's what you've got to do. Give 'em hell if they play you up. It pays in the end, lad. Many a times I've had a row with me mates or the wife, and it's been a comfort to know I've got a real pal down below. If ye cut my veins, Doc, ye'll find fuel oil there, not blood.'

McDougall believed that the best engineers came from Scotland, the best Scots from Glasgow, and the only effect of modern innovations like oil furnaces, engine-room ventilation, and refrigerators was a glaring deterioration in the standard of young men coming to sea. When he showed me round his engine-room he exhibited the reverence of an old dean in his cathedral. We stood on the quivering control platform in the centre of the *Lotus's* clamorous viscera and he waved his arm proudly and shouted, 'This is where we do a man's job, Doc.'

I nodded, looking nervously at the pipes straining with the pressure of superheated steam.

'That's the main steam gauge,' McDougall explained, pointing to a dial on the panel in front of us.

'What's the red line for?' I shouted back.

'That? Och, that's the safety mark.'

'But, I say, isn't the needle well past it?'

'That doesn't matter, lad. We've got to get the old tub moving somehow.'

He took me down greasy ladders, along a narrow cat-walk between pieces of spinning machinery, through the boiler-room where Turnbull, the Geordie Seventh Engineer, sweated eight hours of his twenty-four watching the oil fires. We crouched along the tunnel that carried the propeller shaft to the stern, and stood at the end in a little triangular humid space where the thick revolving metal pierced the plates and disappeared into the sea.

'There ye are, Doc. All us lads and all that machinery to keep this turning. If it wasn't for us that old windbag on the bridge would be out of a job.'

'He doesn't seem to be very appreciative, Chief.'

'Och, we've got better than him conducting the trams in Glasgow,' McDougall said with disgust. 'You watch, Doc, I'll run him off this ship before he's much older. You wait and see.'

McDougall's threat was wholly serious. He had in a locked drawer in his cabin a foolscap book labelled shamelessly HOGG, in which he entered immediately every derogatory fact he discovered about the Captain. When he was particularly annoyed he took the book out and read it, underlining in red ink wherever he thought a passage was not sufficiently condemnatory standing on its own. This book he sent to the Marine Superintendent of the Fathom Line by registered post every time the ship returned to Britain, but its effect was largely cancelled by a similar volume about McDougall put in the Superintendent's hands by the Captain. The two passed their lives in a running fight on oil consumption, engine revolutions, and repair bills, and the daily ceremony by which McDougall handed Captain Hogg a chit on his speed and fuel supplies was always conducted in bitter silence. About once a week the Captain became too much for him, and the Chief Engineer then shut himself in his cabin, took out a fresh bottle of whisky, and determinedly threw the cap through the porthole.

As the ship's company became used to me they paid me the compliment of sharing their troubles with me. I soon discovered all of them were hypochondriacs. In small ships where they had no doctor they worried in case they caught anything; in bigger ships, where there was a doctor living down the alleyway, they brought along their symptoms like bruised children running to their mother. The Second Mate was the severest sufferer from hypochondriasis. The locker in his cabin was a therapeutic bar: he had five different brands of antiseptic, all the popular stomach powders, lotions for rubbing under the arms and between the toes, drops for sticking in his eyes or up his nose, gargles and liniments, hair-food and skin-balm, and a frightening collection of purgatives.

I found him gargling lustily in his cabin one afternoon.

'Hello, Second,' I said. 'What's up? Got a cold?'

He spat guiltily into the basin, as though I had caught him at some wickedness.

'No,' he explained. 'I always gargle three times a day. I was reading an article in *Happy Health* that said every cubic inch of air is loaded with millions of microbes.'

'Well, so's every inch of your throat.'

'Listen, Doc,' he went on, sounding worried. 'There's something I've been wanting to ask you for a long time. Where could I get my blood cholesterol measured?'

'Your what!'

'Yes, you see there was an article in—either the *Reader's Digest* or one of the Sunday papers at home—that said some doctors in California had discovered if your blood cholesterol was above 245 milligrams per cent you were bound to get arteriosclerosis. I've all the symptoms. I . . .'

'You're far more likely to fall down a hatch and break your neck.'

'Do you think so?' he asked eagerly. 'Still, it's got me worried. I'm sure I've got an intervertebral disk as well. There's a pain I get round here in my back every time I sit down.'

'Rubbish! You're healthier than I am.'

He looked dolefully at his medicine chest for a few moments. 'Of course,' he continued, 'what I really need is a woman.'

'I'm inclined to agree with you,' I said.

I sat down reflectively on his bunk. I had become aware in the past few days of feeling—not blatantly sex-starved but unquestionably peckish. I put it down to the sea air. My life ashore had passed undisturbed except for Wendy and occasional vague thoughts that it would be nice to take a girl to the pictures. But now I began to think even the girls in the Third Mate's cabin were delightful. Wendy herself became frighteningly glamourized as my mind's eye behaved like a magazine photographer's lens, and substituted curves for angularity and an inviting expression for the usual one that indicated she thought her nose was running.

'Now, if this was a real passenger ship,' the Second continued, 'everything would be squared up by now. Have you been in one?'

'This is my first ship.'

'I forgot. I was Third in one for a bit. It was like a floating Ball of Kirriemuir. I don't know what it is. As soon as these females get aboard a ship they're all after you. Not a moment's peace. Then there's dances and race meetings and all the fun and games. Not to mention the moonlight and the phosphorescence on the water. I haven't seen any phosphorescence yet. But they fall for it, every time. The places they get to! We found one couple on the steering engine. I used to go under the lifeboats.'

'What about the Captain?'

'He was at it like everyone else. He jacked himself up a nice bit of snicket first day out of Southampton. What a trip that was!'

'I take it you're not married,' I said.

'I've been married. Got hitched during the war when I was a Third. It didn't work out. We've split it up now.' He took a cigarette out of the tin thoughtfully. 'It's no good being married at sea. Oh yes, every leave's a honeymoon, I know what they say. But long voyages and young wives don't mix. You leave the allotment of your pay and if you don't get a letter at every port you wonder what's up. Anyhow, I reckon you can't ask a girl to sit by the fireside for six months, or a year, or two years maybe. It isn't fair. It isn't human.'

'What about you?' I asked.

'Oh, I always hold you're entitled to count yourself as single at sea,' he said.

Our reflections were interrupted by the engine-room telegraph ringing faintly on the bridge above.

'What's that?' I asked. 'I thought they tested them at noon.'

'I expect she's stopped,' Archer said calmly.

'Stopped! But isn't that important?'

'She often stops. It's the first time she's done it this trip. Something's blown up down below, I suppose. Come on deck. From now on it's usually pretty funny.'

We stepped on to the sunny deck, just below the wing of the bridge. The *Lotus* had stopped sure enough. She wallowed in the swell like a dead whale.

'Now watch,' the Second said.

Captain Hogg appeared on the bridge. He had been disturbed in his siesta, and was dressed only in a tartan dressing-gown. He looked like Macbeth the day the wood moved.

'Mr. McDougall!' he shouted. 'Mr. McDougall!'

He banged the rail with his fist.

'Quartermaster! Present my compliments to the Chief Engineer and ask him to come to the bridge!'

'Aye aye, sir.'

Captain Hogg clasped his hands behind him and strode fiercely across the deck. After five minutes McDougall appeared. He was in a boiler-suit and held in his hand a scrap of cotton waste, material that appears as indispensable to engineers as stethoscopes to doctors. They glared across the bridge, playing havoc with each other's blood pressure.

'The ship's stopped,' Captain Hogg announced.

'Aye,' said McDougall. 'I know.'

'Well . . . why the devil has she stopped?'

McDougall lit his pipe.

'You tell me, Cap'n, and then we'll both know.'

'Damn it, Mr. McDougall! Can't you keep the ship going between ports?'

'Not this ship.'

'When I first came to sea engineers took their orders from the bridge. Their job was to raise steam and keep it.'

'When I first came to sea Cap'ns behaved like gentlemen.'

'I will not be spoken to like that!'

'I will speak to ye how I like.'

'I'll have you put in the log-book, Mr. McDougall!'

'I'll report ye to the Company, Cap'n.'

'I will not be obstructed by a pigheaded Scot!'

'An' I will not be told my job by an ignorant Sassenach!'

'Damn you, sir!'

'And damn you, too!'

At that moment the argument was annulled by the telegraph ringing again and the *Lotus* slowly getting under way.

'It's always like that,' the Second said. 'You know how it is. Oil and water won't mix.'

7

THE voyage extended. The ship ran deeply into the Tropics and Captain Hogg started work on his Master's Letter from Santos. We stayed fairly peaceful until the afternoon he threw the Chief Steward down the bridge ladder.

Whimble was the most introverted and anxious member of the *Lotus's* company; and he had a strict rule on board—he never drank. When he came to my cabin early in the voyage and I recalled that the social formulæ of my new life demanded I offered him a peg, he grasped his abdomen with a sigh of horror.

'Not a drop, Doctor!' he declared. 'Never touch a dram of it!'

'What, not at all?' Finding a teetotaller in the *Lotus* was like running into a sober Scot on Burns night.

'Not for twenty years! It's my liver, Doctor.' He warily indicated the region of his umbilicus. 'I had a real bad turn in Cardiff. Five operations and left to die three times. I need say no more to you, need I, Doctor?'

'No, no more at all.'

'So I said to myself, "Walter," I said, "be a man! Not

another drink you're going to have till your dying day!"
And not a drop's soiled my lips since. Will-power, Doctor,
that's what it is. I used to do Pelmanism a bit when I was
younger.'

When I passed this information to Hornbeam, illuminated with admiration, he pushed his cap back on his head
and roared with laughter.

'He's right in a way, Doc,' he said. 'You'll never see him
with a glass in his hand. He keeps it in his locker, mostly.
Or his hot-water can, or under the bunk. He gets a bottle
a day easy—buckshee, of course. Pinches it from the
bond-room and fiddles the bar accounts so it's poor
beggars like you and me that have to pay for it in the end.'

'He cooks the books, does he?' I said in surprise. 'I'd
have thought he was too timid to be dishonest.'

'Don't you believe it. There isn't a chief steward afloat
who wouldn't flog the funnel if he thought he could get
away with it.'

I observed Whimble fairly closely after that. Once
Hornbeam had given me the diagnosis it was simple to
pick out the symptoms. In the early morning, when he did
his round of the galley and the stores, he was a pale and
nervous man who flattened himself against the bulkhead
when he glimpsed Captain Hogg's threatening silhouette
at the other end of the alleyway. At nine he paid his daily
visit to the little bond-room below the water-line, and
came up with the ship's supply of liquor. After that he went
to his cabin to clean his teeth. He reappeared slightly
flushed, and took his place in the inspection procession
with confidence. Then he cleaned his teeth again. He
found it necessary to clean his teeth before dinner, at tea-
time, and on several occasions during the evening. By ten
at night, when he prepared the Captain's sandwiches in

the pantry, his spectacles were awry and he sang snatches of bawdy songs as he slapped on the mustard with a flourish. The end of his day was marked shortly afterwards by the flash of a bottle sailing out of his porthole, and the light splash as it hit the water and joined the others that marked, at neatly regular intervals, the progress of the Chief Steward round the world.

To restore this and other profitable discrepancies, Whimble was forced to spend several hours a day sitting in his tiny office with the store-books and a ready-reckoner, biting his pen and working out worried sums on a scrap of paper.

'Father's very hard, very hard!' he explained to me one day. 'Always chasing me up over the catering. And the Company looks at every grain of rice they give you. What d'you think they'd do if I was a pound of butter out at the end of the voyage?' He indicated the sea with his thumb. 'It would be "Out, Walter, me boy," and no mistake. I don't know how I make ends meet sometimes, really I don't.'

His problem was not so much making ends meet but arranging them to do so with a worthwhile overlap. The drawers under his bunk were filled with tins of ham, peaches, lard, tongue, and pineapple, which were ready to be slipped over the side to a furtive rowing-boat our first night in port. Tins of cigarettes were stacked behind his books in the office, and two or three bottles of whisky were locked in the glass locker with the ostentatious label FOR ENTERTAINMENT OF CUSTOMS. 'If you're wanting any medical stores on the coast, Doc,' he confided in me when I dressed a cut on his hand one evening, 'let me have the list and we'll split the comish fifty-fifty.'

'Very kind of you, I'm sure.'

'Of course, there won't be much in it. There isn't much of anything in this hooker. In a big passenger job that's different. The Purser gets his comish on everything down to the bell-boys' tips. Why, the barman in one of those makes more than the Old Man.' He looked gratefully at his fresh bandage. 'If you want a few bottles of Scotch to flog the other end it might be arranged,' he added generously. 'I can get it ashore for you. Trust Walter. Never touch a drop of it myself, mind you.'

Whimble had justification enough for secret drinking at our expense in the Captain's table manners alone. Captain Hogg made a point of complaining at least once a meal about the menu or cooking. 'Beef!' he would exclaim, contemptuously spitting out a half-chewed morsel as big as a golf ball. 'Flea-ridden cow, more likely! Where the devil did you dig this up from, Mr. Whimble?'

'Fresh on board this trip, sir. Saw it loaded with my own eyes, if I may respectfully say so, sir.'

'I don't believe you, Mr. Whimble. You've had this in the freezer since last voyage, or I'm a Dutchman. What do you say, eh, Doctor?'

As there was no point in disagreeing with the Captain about anything I nodded sympathetically.

When he was especially enraged with a dish Captain Hogg would lift his plate shoulder high, bellow 'Steward!' and demand, 'Throw that muck over the side and bring us a decent piece of bread and cheese.' This he would eat glaring at Whimble, in a silence broken only by the rhythmical snapping of his jaws. On other occasions he would suddenly be overcome with longings, like a pregnant woman. 'Mr. Whimble,' he would demand in the middle of a plate of liver and bacon, 'why don't we ever have any avocado pears?' Or, 'Steward! Are there any pikelets on board?'

After the meagre nourishment of my student's lodgings and the G.P.'s table the portions served in the *Lotus*'s saloon looked heavy with the threat of dyspepsia; but the sea air and the prospect of sleeping all afternoon soon led to my eating as much as anyone else, apart from Captain Hogg. The menu was conservative, like a good commercial hotel's, and ran mostly to joints and puddings. All of them were prepared with care by the First Cook, a large, soft-eyed, likeable man, who sweated among his spitting roasts in the galley whistling and basting the meat with the delight of an esteemed craftsman.

'A contented cook, Doc,' he said, 'and you gets a contented crew.' He whistled a few bars. 'Nice leg of pork cold for supper. Fond of crackling?'

'I'm glad you're contented,' I told him. 'Most of the cooks I meet ashore seem to have duodenal ulcers.'

He wiped his hands on his trousers and felt in his hip pocket.

'That's why I'm contented,' he said. He flourished a photograph of a thin simpering young woman in an off-the-shoulder dance frock. 'Sweetest little girl in the world. That's the wife.'

'You're a very lucky man.'

'Yes, Doc, I reckon I am. One of the luckiest of the lot. How'd you like a bit of dressed crab as well?' he added, glowing with bonhomie. 'I could always open a tin.'

But already, three thousand miles away, disaster was being prepared for the *Lotus*'s cooking. The next afternoon Easter came to my cabin and said, 'Beg pardon, Doctor, but the Cook reckons he wants to do himself in.'

'What! You mean commit suicide?'

'That's right, Doctor. He's been on the booze since dinner, and the lads spotted him rigging up a bit of rope in his cabin.'

'Good Heavens man! Haven't you done something about it?'

'Ho, it's all right now,' Easter said calmly. 'The Bos'n slugged him and he's out cold. He'll be tame enough when he comes to. It's always the same. They never string themselves up in the end.'

'But what's the trouble?' I asked. It seemed barely credible. 'He struck me as a happy enough sort of fellow.'

'Sheilas,' Easter said with contempt. 'Drive a man to it some of them, don't they, Doctor? His wife's vamoosed with a bus-driver. Just got a cable from his pal to say so.'

'That's a bit of tough luck. He seemed to be pretty fond of her.'

'It ain't the first time it's happened by a long chalk. Cor, I've seen these bits waving good-bye to their husbands at the docks, then going home to collect the allotment, a quid a week regular, and ending up with black babies and suchlike. There ain't no depths, Doctor, what women won't stoop to. And the worse they treat the blokes the more they seem to like 'em. Mugs, ain't we?'

'Well, I think you'd better keep an eye on the Cook,' I told him. 'Perhaps I should have a chat with him—psychology, you know. I hope he won't let it interfere with his cooking.'

The next morning was Sunday. The Cook was back at work—but a sad, lonely, tuneless man. He pottered miserably round the galley, pausing every now and then to break into unexpected tears over the carrots or the boiling duff. Suddenly he would cry out startlingly, 'Rosie! Rosie! I love you!' then he would fall silent and look grimly along the edge of his carving-knife, under the terrified glance of the galley-boy who crouched over the potato-bucket.

The Sunday dinner, nevertheless, appeared on the saloon table. Rosie could not have chosen a worse day for her defection, for the menu was the longest of the week: there was always Scotch broth, boiled turbot, steak-and-kidney pie, beef, carrots, boiled and roast potatoes, and plum duff, all of which the Captain consumed steadily and usually without complaint. But that day the Cook's grief had intruded into the meal. The soup was cold, and Captain Hogg flung his spoon into the plate after the first mouthful with the command: 'Steward! Chuck this dishwater into the scupper!' The turbot was underdone, and it was barely touched by anyone. Only the steak-and-kidney pie seemed up to the usual standard. 'Give us a big helping,' the Captain growled. 'If the rest's as filthy as the soup it won't be worth eating. Call yourself a Chief Steward, Mr. Whimble? You're not fit to be in charge of an ice-cream barrow.'

He began eating his pie in silence. We were all a little bad tempered, for Sunday dinner was pleasantly anticipated and we had prepared ourselves with extra morning gin. I watched the Captain sorting out the portions of kidney and felt thankful for the sake of our digestions that peace had fallen on the table.

Captain Hogg suddenly jumped to his feet. He held his napkin to his mouth and his face was the colour of the port light.

'Look!' he hissed. 'Look at that!'

His finger quivered in the direction of his food. Whimble

nervously stretched across the table and removed from a pile of pie-crust a dental plate with three teeth attached to it.

'Oh dear!' Whimble said.

'Is it yours?' the Captain thundered.

'Oh no, sir! I've never seen it before, sir.'

Captain Hogg thrust his napkin forward.

'Put it in that!' he commanded. The teeth, in a pool of gravy, were wrapped up. 'I am taking this up to my cabin and stowing it in the safe. I am then showing it to the general manager the minute we arrive in Liverpool. By God, I'll see you pay for this, Mr. Whimble!'

Shaking his fist he left the saloon, pausing to shout an order for cold ham and pickles in his cabin. We sat in silence, the pie going cold in front of us. Whimble tried to take a drink of water, but he was shaking so much he spilled it over the cloth.

'I don't think I want any more,' Hornbeam said, pushing his plate away. 'Whose are they, Doc? Yours?'

'They're probably the Cook's. He's been a bit forgetful this morning.'

'Har!' Whimble croaked. 'The Cook!' He jumped from the table, eager to pass on his castigation. The gentle, easy-going Cook, who filched tins of ham and corned beef through Whimble's good graces, was the only person on board whom he could bully. Pausing only to clean his teeth on the way, he confidently made for the galley.

But it was a changed Cook whom he found sitting on the potato locker with a gin-bottle, crooning to himself. He saw the accident in a different light. Before Whimble could say anything he was gripped by the shirt, a chopping-knife pointed at his throat, and the Cook demanded 'Give me my bloody teeth back!'

Whimble broke away with a shout that brought us all

from the saloon. We found him running down the deck chased by the Cook, who had his knife in his hand and was wearing a frightening toothless snarl.

'Murder!' Whimble shouted.

The Cook was not steady on his feet, fell over a stay, and burst into tears. But Whimble had no time to see this. His only thoughts were of self-protection, and he decided the unpleasantness represented by Captain Hogg was less than that embodied in the Cook. He jumped up the ladder leading to the bridge and hammered on the door of the Captain's cabin.

'Help!' he cried. 'Save me!'

The door was flung open.

'What the blazes is the matter with you?'

'Look,' said Whimble, pointing behind him.

'Are you mad!'

'The Cook's after me with a knife!' he whimpered, calming at the sight of Captain Hogg. 'He wants his teeth back.'

'Teeth! Teeth! Did you say teeth? Get off my bridge!'

'He'll murder me!'

'Get off my bridge, damn you!'

'Give me the cook's teeth first!'

Captain Hogg picked Whimble up by his shirt collar and gave him a push. He uttered a little squeal as he lost his balance at the top of the ladder and came sliding down feet first. At that moment the steward was mounting it with the Captain's tray of ham and pickles.

'There goes our supper,' Hornbeam said gloomily. After that no one thought it worth while finishing the meal.

8

THE next morning my professional tranquility was split like an old sail in a storm.

I had settled down in my cabin after breakfast to read *War and Peace*, with which I first killed three or four cockroaches, when Easter came in. He showed me a new card trick and described the occasion when he was steward on a Greek tramp and had won from the skipper, an incorrigible but luckless gambler, as a final stake one night in the Mediterranean the exclusive services of his stout but agreeable wife until Gibraltar.

'There's something, Doctor,' Easter went on. 'One of the crew took queer in the night.'

'What's wrong with him?'

'Vomiting and suchlike. Shall I chase him up here?'

'I think we'd better pay a domiciliary visit.'

The patient was a young deckhand. He was lying on his bunk, holding his abdomen and groaning.

'Good morning,' I said briskly, taking his pulse. 'What's the trouble?'

'Aw, cripes! I got the bellyache something horrid.'

'Just let me have a look at the—er, stomach.'

He stretched himself on his back. I reached out a hand and felt the right-hand quadrant of his abdomen. Immediately I felt as if I had eaten a bunch of safety-pins and they had all opened inside at once.

I dragged Easter outside the door and shut it.

'Easter,' I said hoarsely. 'This man has acute appendicitis.'

'Cor!'

'This is urgent. How far are we out of Santos?'

'About two days, the Mate reckons.'

'Well, we must make land before then and put the poor chap in hospital. I'll go up and see the Captain.'

Captain Hogg had just got out of his bath. He stood in his slippers with a towel round him, looking at me like Bligh offering Christian the cheese. I could appreciate that it was one of his gastric mornings.

'Well?'

'Er—good morning, sir.'

'Good morning!'

'Could you do twice the speed you are, sir?'

'What!'

He jumped so violently he shook drops of water from his chest on to the carpet.

'I mean—you see, sir, one of the crew has developed acute appendicitis. He will have to be operated on as soon as possible. I understand from the engineers that it is possible for the vessel to make a few more knots, and I thought . . .'

Captain Hogg sat down on the edge of his desk. He gave a sharp tug to his left ear, as though pulling the pin out of a Mills bomb.

'For every knot above the cruising speed of my ship,' he began quietly, 'the bill for fuel oil practically doubles itself. What do you think the Company would have to say? Eh?' He banged the desk. 'Operate, Doctor, operate!' he shouted. 'What do you think I pay you for?'

'Yes, sir,' I said.

I recognized at once that the Captain's advice on therapy had obvious drawbacks. In the first place, I had a meagre idea of how to remove an appendix. A medical qualification is like a marriage licence—it gives you official permission to go ahead, but it doesn't guarantee you know enough to tackle all the difficulties after the honeymoon. I had diligently attended the operating theatre in my hospital, but there were always so many students present whenever the surgeons removed an appendix that all I usually saw of the operation were the boils on the neck of the man in front of me.

The second difficulty was equipment. Although appendices have reportedly been removed by second mates with bent spoons and a bos'n's knife, I felt that my academic inhibitions made it impossible for me to operate skilfully with the products of an ironmonger's shop. Thirdly, there was professional assistance. Easter was an admirable character for whom I had a sincere admiration as a man of the world, but when it came to dabbling in clinical medicine he was as dangerous as an unlabelled bottle of strychnine.

I called him into my cabin.

'Easter,' I said earnestly, 'have you seen a case of acute appendicitis before?'

'Ho, yes, Doctor. Every time I eats pickles I'm reminded of it.'

'Pickles?'

'That's right, Doctor. I was on the Western Ocean run

at the time. The old Doc was scared to operate, so he puts the patient in the ship's hospital and tells me to keep him on a light diet, see. That night I goes along and asks if there's anything he wants, like, before I turn in, and the patient says to me "Yes," he says, "I should like just a few pickles." "Pickles!" I says. "You can't have no pickles! Don't be balmy! The Doctor would have me over the side if I was to give you pickles. We of the medical fraternity don't reckon pickles is a light diet. Not for 'arf a minute we don't," I says.'

'Well the next morning I brings him 'is breakfast—two poached eggs done special—and when I goes to shake him—Cor! He was cold to the touch. Them pickles was his last wish, Doctor, and I refused him. Sad, ain't it?'

'Quite so, Easter,' I said. 'Let's have a little less of your reminiscences and a little more action. We must operate on this man before sundown. Do you realize what that means? We must strip the hospital, scrub it out with antiseptic, rig up some lights and an operating table, and find some instruments from somewhere. Savvy?'

'Very good, Doctor. We of the fraternity always rises to the occasion, as they say.'

'Well, start rising.'

He hesitated.

'If I might be so bold, Doctor . . .'

'Yes?'

'Perhaps it might make things go a little easier if you and me was to have a bit of the medical comforts to start with.'

I clapped him gratefully on the shoulder.

'Capital idea, Easter. Reach down the bottle from my locker.'

D

Rumours of my intended surgical assault spread through the ship faster than the news of a landfall. It was not only a pleasurable interruption to the tedium of the voyage but it had the attributes of mystery and originality as well. The crew hadn't had such fun since a boiler blew up off Panama.

I shut myself in my cabin and opened the text-book of surgery I had prudently included in my packing. Turning over the pages to appendicitis, I ran my finger down the print. I started to read the section headed 'operation.' 'The incision is made at McBurney's point,' it said. Oh God! What was McBurney's point? It sounded like a mountain in California.

There was a rap on the jalousie.

'Come in!'

I unlatched the door. It was the Chief Engineer.

'I heard about this wee party you're having, Doc,' he said affably. 'I reckoned you'd be needing some lights so's you can get a good squint at the innards. I can rig up a cargo cluster for you, if you're willing.'

'Thanks very much.'

He gave a grin.

'Of course, you won't mind me turning up to see the fun, Doc, will you? I reckon I ought to be there in case the lights go on the blink. You never can tell with these cargo clusters.'

'That'll be all right, Chief.'

'Thanks, Doc. Give us a shout when you want to stand-by.'

I opened the book again, and had read far enough to learn that the appendix may be in any of six positions when Hornbeam put his head round the door. He laughed loudly.

'Hello, Doc! Making you do a bit of work for a change?'

'That's what I'm here for,' I said casually.

'Reading it all up in the old almanac, I see,' he said genially.

I shut the heavy book with a bang and dropped it behind the bunk.

'One must refresh one's memory,' I said. 'Even Lord Lister had to do that sometimes.'

'What I came down for, Doc,' he went on, 'was to offer you a bit of a hand. I remember seeing one of these done in the war when I was trooping. Thought you might like me to hold the blood-bucket or something.'

I considered.

'All right,' I said. 'I'd be pleased to have someone with common-sense around. You won't faint, will you?'

'What, after all these years at sea? I'll come along later.'

I was still looking for my place in the surgery book when I saw Sparks in the doorway. He brushed aside a couple of imaginary companions and grinned at me.

'Yes?' I asked uninvitingly.

'I hear you're going to carve 'em up, Doc.'

'I am intending to operate, certainly.'

'Wouldn't mind if I watched, would you? I'm a bit of a photographer, and I'd like a few pictures to show the kids.' His grin widened. 'Makes a change from sea-gulls.'

'I don't think there'll be enough room for me and the patient if you come too.'

'Would you like to send a message to his mother?' he asked.

'No, I would not.'

'Haven't got a spot of gin handy, have you?'

'Not now. Later. I'm very busy.'

'All right, Doc. Have a good time.'

He went off, singing with his friends. But there had now collected outside the door a bunch of deckhands, led by the Bos'n with his cap respectfully in his hands.

'What the hell do you want?' I asked crossly.

'Sorry to disturb you, Doctor, only seeing as we're all pals of Erb's, we was thinking you'd let us come in, see, to 'ave a dekko. 'E says it's all right wiv 'im, as long as we behaves decent.'

'Go away,' I said. 'Go away at once. All of you. Who do you think I am? A music-hall turn? I shall report you all to the Mate.'

I slammed the door and returned to the intricacies of appendicectomy.

*   *   *   *

I found Easter in the hospital. He had dismantled the cabin furnishings and was on his knees scrubbing the deck, stripped to the waist.

'How's it going?' I asked.

'It's bloody 'ot.'

'What's the temperature?'

He got up and inspected the thermometer in the corner.

'Hundred and six,' he said.

'Can't you put the forced draught on?'

'Blows soot in.'

'Oh, all right. We'll have to put up with it I suppose. How have you got on with the operating table?'

He had a wooden trestle table along one bulkhead,

which he set up proudly. It left just enough room on
either side for the pair of us.

'I got it off Chippy,' he said. 'He uses it for mixing the
paints on.'

'It's better than nothing. If you scrub it hard enough
it'll be reasonably sterile.'

As I spoke, two large, rusty drops fell from a pipe
crossing the deckhead on the spot where the operation
wound would be.

'Damnation! Can't you do anything to stop that?'

Easter shook his head.

'Been like it for years. It's a job for the shore engineers,
that is.'

'Well, you'll have to fix up some sort of screen. Have
we got any dressings and gloves, and so forth?'

'There was some in the locker. Seem to have been there
since the war.'

'Get them sterilized in the galley. How about instruments? What have you found?'

Easter pulled two handfuls of metal objects from his
trouser pockets.

'I've been on the scrounge,' he explained. 'I thought
these would come in handy, like.'

I looked at his booty, which he spread on the table.
There was a pair of pliers, two saloon forks, a packet of
darning needles labelled 'A Sailor's Friend,' some paper-
clips, a stiletto, a potato knife, a pair of tweezers, a
surgical scalpel, and a uterine curette.

'You'd better sterilize the lot,' I said gloomily. 'Except
the pliers. Shouldn't there be a set of surgical instruments
on board?'

'They seem to have disappeared, Doctor.'

'You mean you flogged them?' He scratched his nose

guiltily. 'There's nothing for it but to use what we've got,' I told him crossly. 'I damn well hope you get an appendix, too!'

I went out on deck. I needed some fresh air. The day was already becoming too much for me.

Outside the hospital I found Chippy. He was sitting on the deck with a hatch cover—a thick piece of wood about six feet by two used in rows to cover the hatches. He was polishing it carefully with emery paper.

'Hello, Chips,' I said. 'Getting everything shipshape for Santos?'

He looked up at me gloomily.

'He'll slide off this lovely,' he said.

'Who will?'

'Why—'im down there.' He pointed aft with his thumb. 'The poor bloke what's for the knife. Slide off it like a wet fish, he will,' he added with relish.

I was perplexed.

'What's he want to slide off a hatch cover for?' I asked.

'Why, when they buries 'im, of course.' He gave it another rub. 'Lot of work I've put in on this 'ere 'atch cover.'

'Now, look here, Chippy. What gives you the idea my patient's going to die?'

'Oh, they always does. I've seen five appendicitises at sea. 'Ad their time, every one of 'em. Over the wall they went on a 'atch cover.'

I stamped off in disgust. I felt I had been professionally insulted. I climbed the bridge ladder angrily to report the Carpenter's pessimism to one of the Mates. There I found the Second moodily sorting out flags.

'What ho, Doc,' he said. 'When's the carve-up?'

'In about an hour.'

'Think that ensign'll do?'

'Do? What for?'

'Why, in case—in case of accidents. To cover the body.'

'There isn't going to be any body, damn you!'

'Well, Father told us to take precautions. Means a lot of work for all hands, Doc. It'll be a shame if they're all disappointed now.'

I admit that they do give one an excellent funeral at sea. The properties are traditionally adapted from the ship's gear and the routine is prescribed as firmly as that for entering and leaving port. As soon as the body is available it is turned over to the bos'n, who sews it up in canvas with half a dozen firebars from the galley. For this he receives a bottle of whisky. Meanwhile, the carpenter has been polishing and attaching rope handles to a hatch cover, and the quartermasters have been pressing their best uniforms. The ceremony is held at sunset or sunrise on the same day, because ships spend most of their time in tropical waters and the performance might be marred by the corpse if it became aggressively high. The vessel stops, a rail is taken away from the side, and the ship's officers, including the abashed Doctor, line up with the Captain. Caps are removed, and at the appropriate moment the body is marched to the rails on the hatch cover by the quartermasters—who receive a bottle of whisky between them for their services—and smartly tipped overboard. The Mate, who has charge of all deck stores including flags, at the same time edges himself down to the rail and grabs the ensign—which costs the Company money—before it slips into the sea with its bundle. The ship then starts again and everyone goes off for an obituary peg.

'I should hate to spoil your fun,' I said coldly, 'but this patient is going to walk off the ship in Liverpool.'

I returned into the hospital, where Easter was boiling the instruments over a Primus stove.

'Everyone thinks there's going to be a funeral,' I said. 'I never heard such nonsense.'

'Ho, yes,' Easter remarked calmly. 'That's why I couldn't fit a screen under that there pipe as you said. Bos'n says he's got to keep all his spare canvas for the shroud.'

'But it's monstrous!'

Easter chuckled over the steaming instruments.

'Cor, I've seen some funny funerals at sea! Remember one we had in the Indian Ocean. Chinaman it was. Got knifed. Blimey, we pushed him overboard all right, but he wouldn't sink. Bobbed about like a buoy. The Old Man wasn't 'arf flummoxed. In the end we had to leave him to it. Couldn't pull him out again, could we? Probably still bobbing about somewhere, if the sharks ain't got him.'

'I'm going to see the patient,' I said sternly. 'Get everything ready in an hour's time.'

The patient was sitting in his cabin eating fish and chips and drinking a bottle of beer.

'What the devil's this!' I shouted. 'I thought I told you to have nothing by mouth?'

'Oh, sorry, Doc,' he said awkwardly. 'But seeing I was feeling so much better like, I thought I could do with a bit of grub.'

'Better, man! How dare you say you're better! That's for me to decide. You only think you're better. You've got an acute appendix inside you.'

He pulled a fish bone out of his mouth repentantly.

'There's just one thing, Doc,' he said respectfully. 'Do people often get this appendix taken out twice.'

'Twice? What do you mean?'

'Well, I had it taken out the first time in Birkenhead when I was six . . .'

I sprang at him and pulled up his shirt. A faint, white two-inch scar. I started to laugh.

*   *   *   *

'Not operating, Doctor? Why?' Captain Hogg demanded.

'I've charmed it away, sir,' I explained. 'A trick I learnt in infancy from a gypsy.'

9

WE arrived at Santos in the early afternoon. As we slowed down to approach the river mouth between the deep green hills the shore heat hit us like the blast from the engine-room hatchway.

'It'll be nice and cosy alongside,' Easter said gloomily.

We sailed up the greasy river between the rows of ships tied thickly along each bank, the ensign of the United States of Brazil flying in courtesy from our foremast. Hornbeam went to his station forrard, and Archer took the Lamptrimmer and his gang of deckhands aft. The tugs came up, the mooring ropes flew out, and we were pushed into place as neatly as a well-parked car. The gangway rattled down and a section of the rail was pulled away: we had arrived.

But we were still flying the yellow Q flag, indicating we were in quarantine. A troop of stout Brazilian customs and health officials immediately tramped aboard, headed by an important-looking man in a white suit whom I took to be the Doctor.

I saluted.

'Boa dia, senhor,' I said in carefully incubated Portuguese.

He held out his hand.

'Afternoon, old boy,' he replied. 'How's tricks?'

'Very well, thank you.'

'Nothing infectious?'

'No.'

'Haul down the yellow peril, then. Can you let me have a few hundred English cigarettes?'

Once the quarantine flag was down people came aboard like Navy Week visitors on a bank holiday. There were policemen, stevedores, money-changers, ship chandlers, water purveyors, fruit sellers, harbourmasters, launderers— and the agents. The agents were the men in charge of the Fathom Line's business in Santos, and could get any commodity at short notice from five thousand tons of oil to a new bell for the ship's cat. They were a pair of tall genial Englishmen with minds like efficiently arranged shopping lists.

'Hello, Doc,' one said. 'Want any medical stores?'

'Chief Steward's got the list.'

'Good. You've taken over from Flowerday, have you? He was a rum bird. Coming to have a peg?'

'Not just now.'

'Fair enough. By the way, there's some mail for you somewhere.'

I had forgotten that the agents look after the ship's mail. I went out on deck and found most of it had been distributed. All over the ship men were leaning on uncomfortable steel corners reading their letters. I passed the Carpenter, who had several closely-written sheets in his hand and kept saying 'No! It can't be! It can't be!' to himself. I hoped it was nothing serious.

'Coo!' one man shouted. 'I've 'ad a baby!'

'I've 'ad six,' his companion said morosely, not looking up. This nonplussed the new father.

'Wot, all at once?' he asked.

I ran into Whimble.

'Letter for you, Doc,' he said. 'I gave it to Easter.'

I suddenly felt excited. I had forgotten England and home in the past three weeks as efficiently as a patient with amnesia. My past seemed a disconnected existence. All at once I felt a letter would be like a familiar face in a big crowd.

I saw Easter leaning on the rail and hurried towards him. I wondered who it was from. Wendy, perhaps? Telling me she was crying over my picture and reading Conrad? From my principal, genially wishing me a good voyage? Or my parents, asking where I'd put the keys of the garage? From old classmates envious of my double release? I didn't care. It was a letter, a letter. Whoever sent it proved the most important thing in the world—I was not forgotten.

I took the envelope from Easter. I couldn't recognize the handwriting. I tried to open it with dignity, but excitedly tore the flap. It said: '*The——— Laundry. Dear Sir, If you do not collect your washing within seven days of this date it will be sold to defray charges.*'

I tossed it into the dock. I leant on the rail and looked at the unfamiliar colours, the dirty yellow sheds, the strange un-English mountains in the background with the white road wriggling up them to São Paulo, the dusky lounging men and slim graceful women on the wharfside, the signs in Portuguese, the odd open tramcar behind, the surprising uniforms of the police, the glare of the unaccustomed sun . . . I realized tardily I was on another side of the world.

*   *   *   *

After conditioning myself to the exclusive company of my shipmates for three weeks I found the rush of locals on board unsettling. The silence of the sea passage was broken by the noise of the winches, and the bare decks became littered with hatch covers, wires, tarpaulins, pieces of dropped cargo, and resting Brazilians. The Brazilians have a great capacity for rest. When they have nothing to do for a few minutes they see no point in continuing to support the burden of keeping awake and fling themselves into the nearest piece of shade. Whether they are lying on a stone wharf, the top of a couple of packing-cases, or some pieces of scrap metal does not appear to detract from the enjoyment.

The cargo came out by the exact reverse of the technique that put it in at Liverpool. As I had nothing else to do I joined Easter, who was watching crates of machinery being drawn out of number five hatch with the pleasantly indolent air of a Londoner observing road excavations.

'Hope you've locked your cabin, Doctor,' he said. 'And screwed up the port. These boys would pinch the soles off your shoes if you wasn't careful.'

I pointed towards the policemen on the gangway.

'But don't they keep an eye on it?'

'What, them vigilantes? Them's the worst of the lot.'

As the winches paused I heard feminine giggles and zestful screams coming from the crew's quarters in the poop. A plump dark girl with a basket of washing under her arm appeared on the deck, struggling formally with a large sailor.

'That's Maria,' Easter explained. 'She does your

laundry for you. Three blokes got something off her last trip.'

'What!'

'Wouldn't mind having a go at her myself,' he continued solemnly. 'They don't seem to think much of things like that out here. All the girls is tenderhearted. I reckon it's the climate.'

'It all seems very unhygienic to me, to say the least.'

'Mind you, some of 'em's real smashers. Ho, I've had some fun here, I have. You going ashore to-night, Doctor?'

'I might stretch my legs. Though I fear I shall do nothing more exciting than go to the pictures.'

'Ah, you can get some queer pictures out here too,' Easter went on. 'Pal of mine went ashore one night to have his pleasure, as you might say, and the next day he went off with a crowd of the lads to one of them odd picture houses. Blimey, he was the big feature. Didn't 'arf get his leg pulled about it.'

'I think I will go and see Mr. Hornbeam,' I said. Santos sounded a place that would have provided Easter with extensive reminiscences.

Hornbeam's cabin was as full as a compartment in a suburban train in the rush-hour. There were the agents, the chief stevedores, the customs, the immigration officers, and a few unidentifiable officials. Hornbeam was sitting with his white shirt undone to the waist, looking pleased with himself. His table was filled with bottles of gin, whisky, and beer, and half a dozen open tins of Players. Everyone was helping themselves.

'Come in, Doc!' he called. 'Have a peg. This is our Doctor, gentlemen.'

'How do you do,' I said, taking a glass.

'It's always open house in the Mate's cabin in port,' Hornbeam explained, pouring himself another gin. 'Everyone wants the poor bloody Mate. Now what about 'this trouble in number three?' he said to the head steve-dore. 'Can you get another gang on there to-night?'

'To-morrow morning, Mister Mate. To-night, no good.'

'We'll have to put up with it, I suppose.'

He took a sheaf of papers from a ragged Brazilian who appeared in the doorway.

'Cargo plans? All right. Have a peg, chum. Coming ashore to-night, Doc?' he added to me.

'I thought of it. Are you?'

'Certainly I am. Never been ashore in Santos yet. To-night I am. We'll collect here about midnight. . . .'

'Midnight?'

'There's no point in going anywhere before eleven in this part of the world. Nothing livens up before twelve.'

"If that's the case I think I'd better turn in for a bit.'

'That's the idea, Doc. You're in the land of the siesta now, don't forget. God, it's hot, isn't it?'

*   *   *   *

I screwed the closely-meshed wire-netting in the port-hole to keep the flies out and went to sleep. The Second woke me up about nine.

'Coming ashore?' he asked. 'We're going up to the Mate's cabin. They sting you for drinks in Brazil so we reckoned we'd get a glow on us before we went off.'

I sat up and rubbed the sweat off me with a sheet.

'I'll be up when I've had a shower. The Mate's coming with us, isn't he?'

Archer laughed.

'I wouldn't know about that. I've never seen him get ashore anywhere yet.'

When I reached the Mate's cabin I saw at once that he had not been taking a siesta himself. His visitors had gone and the bottles were empty. He sat behind a jumble of dirty glasses and cigarette-ends, humming absently to himself.

' 'Lo, Doc,' he said languidly. 'Fetch a bottle out of the locker there. I'm coming ashore with you young lads to-night. Keep you out of trouble, eh? Muy bien. Cheerio.'

Archer and Trail were in the cabin, dressed in their shore-going rig. The scattered places in which they bought their clothes and their over-compensation for wearing uniform most of their lives gave them a startling appearance. Trail was particularly arresting. He wore a pair of green cotton trousers he had bought in Rio, a yellow shirt from Calcutta, the sort of sports coat that is, fortunately, popular only on the Australian beaches, suede shoes from Ceylon, and a tie with a luminous girl on it from New York.

We all sat down and drank determinedly.

'Have to drink beer ashore,' Trail said. 'A gin costs about twelve bob. I got some cruzeiros for you, Doc.' He handed me a bundle of dirty notes. 'That's the sub you put in for. How about you, Mr. Hornbeam?'

'Got some in the kitty,' he said thickly.

He pulled a tin out of his locker and spilt the contents on the table. There was currency from all over the world— Australian florins, South African sixpences, nickels and quarters, escudos and francs, Canadian dollars, Japanese yen, New Zealand pounds, rupees, pesos, pesetas, and guilders, a few marks, and a couple of Pitcairn Island postage stamps.

'Always like to have a bit of ready cash,' he explained, rummaging through the pile. 'No cruzeiros, though. What's this?' He held up a coin and squinted at it. 'Springbok ha'penny. No good. I'll take the dollars ashore and flog 'em. Don't you blokes go without me,' he added threateningly. 'I'll get a cob on if you don't wait. Where are we bound for, anyway? Have another peg.'

The Third drew a small book from his pocket and turned over to the letter S.

'Santos . . .' he said. 'Oh, that's fixed. We'll take the Doc to the Whores' Ball.'

'The what did you say?' I asked.

'The Whores' Ball. Funniest thing this side of the Line. It doesn't start till midnight. We'll look into the Ritz Bar first.'

'I want to see the Bidu Bar,' Archer added. 'I met a hot bit of blonde in there last time.'

'You game, Doc?'

By this time my critical faculties were mildly blunted with gin.

'Game? Of course I'm game. I'm a sailor, aren't I?'

'That's the spirit!' Trail said. 'Down the hatch, lads, and let's get moving. It's after eleven.'

'What about the Mate?' I asked. I turned to look at him. He was lying with his head in a pool of currency asleep.

'It's always the same with the Mate,' Archer explained. 'He never makes it. Hasn't been ashore for years. It's best to leave him there until he wakes up. Now for the bright lights!' Trail put down his glass. 'Come on, Doc!'

Singing softly we filed down the gangway and, slightly intoxicated, for the first time in my life I put foot on foreign soil.

10

THERE are few attractive cities in Brazil, and Santos is not one of them. In the centre is a fairly pleasant square with gardens in it, a new post office, and the Town Hall. It would pass for a little bastion of bourgeoisie in the South of France on a hot day. But the waterfront caters, efficiently, for different tastes. It is a tall line of buildings on a cobbled street that looks like the slums in Glasgow draped with neon.

The Third led us jauntily towards a lighted doorway with RITZ BAR—DRINKS AND GIRLS shining over it.

'Here we go lads!' he said. 'If our mothers could see us now!'

The three of us piled inside and took a table by the door. It was a long room, brightly lit, with a bar down one side, a small dance floor, and a band. The walls were lined with foreign flags and signs such as WELCOMES TO OUR BRITISH FRIENDS, HAVE A SWELL TIME BABY, and WE TAKE POUNDS AND DOLLARS. The room was full, but not with Brazilians. There seemed to be sailors there from every country with a seaboard. There were stiff blond Swedes and Norwegians, a crowd

of drunk Greeks in the corner, some Dutchmen, a pack of
Frenchmen arguing with Spaniards, blank-faced masti-
cating Americans, and a good many small dark-eyed
dangerous-looking men of unplaceable nationality. By the
door, stroking his long moustache, stood a nervous
Brazilian policeman.

'I say!' I exclaimed. I stared at the place like a child
brought up to Town to see the lights. 'It looks a bit
tough, doesn't it?'

'The Santos waterfront is the toughest in the world,'
Archer said lightly. 'That's why we're sitting near the
door. If anything starts don't wait to see what it's all
about, but hop it. They have a habit of arresting everyone
in sight down here. Ever been in jail?'

'Not yet.'

'This isn't the place to start. I got pinched two years
ago for being drunk. They let me go next morning,
luckily. Had to rub shoulders with some pretty queer
birds. None of this single cell and bath business you get in
Britain.'

A Brazilian girl, dark and rounded, in a black dress and
a decorative lace apron came upon us.

'Três cerveja,' Trail said.

'Sure, baby.'

She strolled off, giving us the benefit of her hips.

'She brings the beer,' Trail explained. 'If you like you
can dance with her. Look over there.'

There were about twenty of the girl's colleagues in the
room, all similarly dressed. I watched one at the table
next to ours being asked for a dance by an American, who
used the technique of slapping her on the bottom and
grabbing her arm as she passed. The girl smiled acquies-
cence, and they took the floor.

The band played only sambas and rumbas. The polite versions of these dances produced in London restaurants have the same relationship to Santos sambas as vintage Burgundy to raw applejack. Similarly with the dancing. The Brazilian girls, though languid in daytime, come to life like flashing electric signs at nightfall. Not only do they dance lustily, but they do so without any inhibitions whatever. If any couple in London were seen performing in the manner accepted as normally sociable in Brazil, they would be immediately asked to leave.

The girl brought our beers and opened them. Trail handed her a hundred-cruzeiro note and pinched her bottom. She grinned at him. I wondered what would have happened if he had tried the same technique in a Lyons' teashop.

'Don't reckon we'll stay here long,' Trail said. 'It's getting on. How do you like Brazilian beer?'

'It tastes like soapy water to me.'

'It carries a kick in it somewhere. Finish it up, we've got to look in at the Bidu.'

'Saw a chap get killed outside there last trip,' Archer said to me.

The Bidu Bar was exactly the same as the Ritz except that the signs round the walls were in Portuguese and the girls were fatter.

We didn't stay long. We had a couple more beers and left. Trail rubbed his hands. 'And now,' he said, 'for the Whores' Ball.'

The function to which Trail was so attracted was held on the top floor of an old building on one of the side streets. We could hear the music, the inescapable samba, blaring down the street from the open windows before we turned the corner. The way in was through a narrow door with TAXI DANCING painted over the top of it and up a long, narrow, unbroken flight of stairs. At the foot of the stairs was a ticket office, inside which a fat man in his vest was barred up like the crown jewels.

We paid, and mounted the staircase. At the top were two solemn policemen, who immediately advanced on us. Archer's remarks about the carelessness of the police in arresting people flashed into my mind. I jumped nervously and began to walk backwards down the stairs.

'Don't be alarmed,' Archer said. 'In England you leave your hat and coat, don't you?'

By that time a policeman had grabbed hold of me, pulled aside my arms, and searched me for weapons. I caught sight of a table behind him that explained Archer's remarks. On it was neatly arranged a collection of revolvers, knives, blackjacks, knuckle-dusters, and razors.

'The Brazilian likes going around with a bit of cutlery in his belt,' Trail explained. 'Makes him feel big. Unfortunately he tends to be a bit on the excited side. These cops sometimes miss a knife or two, so we'd better keep near the windows. Don't mind a jump, do you?'

We went inside. Three girls immediately came up to us and told us they loved us. Trail waved them aside. 'We came to hear the music,' he told them affably.

We strode across the floor and sat down. It was bigger than the American Bar and had more space for dancing. The walls were bare of any decoration and the floor was rough boards polished only by the customers' feet. There were tables scattered round the floor, and girls scattered round the tables. The atmosphere was like a laundry with a breakdown in the ventilating system.

At one end was the band—on a platform six feet above the floor and surrounded by barbed wire.

'What's the barricade for?' I asked.

'If they dislike the music here they don't hide their feelings,' Trail explained.

'What about all these girls? What do they do?'

'If you pay fifty cruzeiros you'll find out.'

'Oh, I see. Let's have some beer.'

We sat and drank and watched the dancing. It was the sort that Trail described as 'the bumps and grinds.' I looked nervously at men sitting at the other tables, with an expectant sensation between my shoulder-blades. When they saw a girl they fancied they grabbed her and joined the jactitating couples on the floor. After the dance they either went off with her, dragged her back to their own tables, or left her, according to the strength of their inclination. I saw a party of our Liverpool greasers in the corner, their shirts unbuttoned and outside their trousers, throwing Merseyside witticisms at their neighbours. Everyone seemed to be having a good time.

A warm brunette descended on my knee.

'Hallo darling!' she said. 'You come wit' me?'

'No!'

She laughed and ruffled my hair.

'You dance wit' me, no?'

'Go on, Doc,' Archer called. 'Give the girls a treat.'

'But I can't dance.'

'Come on, darling,' said the girl. She snatched hold of me and pulled me out of my chair. Then she clapped me to her bosom like a belladonna plaster and pushed me on the dance floor.

We jostled with the rest of the dancers. It was like being lashed to an upholstered pneumatic drill. I struggled round

in her clammy embrace, trying to keep my feet, wriggling
out of other men's way, and reflecting that I was a long
way from home.

When the music stopped I disengaged myself and looked
for our table. By this time the Third was talking earnestly
to a thin, brown girl who had taken my chair.

'Thirty cruzeiros,' he said forcefully. 'Trinta. See?' He
held up three fingers.

She shook her head. 'No!' she insisted. 'Cincoenta.
Fifty, fifty, fifty!'

'Oh hell,' the Third said. 'Let's get out of here.'

We trooped down the stairs. 'Where now?' Archer asked
when we were in the street.

'Madame Mimi's,' Trail said with finality. 'It's the only
place where you can get a decent bottle of beer in town.'

'I think I'm going back to the ship,' I said.

'Come on, Doc! You don't have to sample the goods.
Besides you'd get knifed walking back alone. Where is it,
Second? Somewhere near the Rua Bittencourt, I think ...'

He led us along threatening unlighted streets, where the
pedestrians shuffled guiltily in the shadows like large
rats.

'I think this is the number,' he said, stopping by the
heavy door of an unlighted house. 'You fellows stay here
and I'll go and see.'

He jumped up the steps and rang the bell. After a
minute or so I saw him jab it again. The door opened.
An old woman with her hair tied in a handkerchief stood
against the inside light.

'Boa noite, senhora,' Trail began. He held a conversation in Portuguese with her, and I saw that he spoke
the language rapidly and with great force, but unin-
telligibly. After he had delivered a string of sentences

embellished heavily with gestures she held up a finger and disappeared to fetch help. A tall man in a dressing-gown came back with her. After a few words he pushed the Third abruptly down the steps, delivered a few hostile sentences, and slammed the door.

'Wrong place,' Trail explained, picking himself up. 'That seems to be the dentist's. It must be the house on the other corner.'

At the next door we were received with pleasure and shown immediately into the parlour.

Madame Mimi's was a sedate establishment. The parlour was furnished in the austere, grubby style popular with the Continental middle-class; it was a large apartment with big shuttered windows, containing several small tables and a larger one in the corner where Madame sat with three or four of her charges. On a dark, broken sideboard down one side were two unlighted candelabras, a sickly-looking plant, and a radio. Round the walls were pictures of the saints. Business was poor, and the room was quiet and inactive. One felt one had called on the vicar's daughters for tea.

Madame immediately recognized my companions and greeted them warmly.

'Ah, hello my little boys! Back so soon, eh? How goes it in cold England?'

She embraced the two of them. She was a big, over-powdered woman in a black dress, with a figure like a thawing snowman.

'Not so dusty,' Archer said. 'Meet one of our shipmates.' We embraced.

'Madame is a wonderful character,' Trail explained. 'Hails from France originally. She built up her own team here like a football manager.'

'Now, boys,' Madame said. 'You would like some beer, no?'

'Lay it on, Madame,' Archer said, sitting down and slapping his knee. 'Lay on everything.'

Madame clapped her hands.

'Is that little girl Dina still here?' Trail asked.

Our hostess shrugged her shoulders powerfully.

'She is gone. She married a gentleman from São Paulo.'

'Well, he hasn't done badly,' Trail observed. 'Let's have a look at the latest talent.'

Madame's assistant brought the tall green beer bottles and glasses, and three girls came over to sit with us. They were pretty girls—slim, dainty, smiling, glowing with co-operation.

'Americano?' asked the one next to me eagerly.

'No. Ingles.'

'Cigarette?' she asked, as winsomely as a schoolgirl appealing for pocket money. I gave her one, which she put carefully in her handbag. She began to stroke the back of my neck. I clasped my hands in front of me and stared defensively at the opposite wall.

'I lof you,' she said.

We sat like that for some time. Meanwhile, Trail and Archer had their girls on their knees and were conducting a conversation in a mixture of English, Portuguese, and giggles.

'You come with me?' the girl asked, playfully pulling a hair from my neck.

'No,' I said. 'I—I não gostar, or whatever it is. Nothing doing. Go and talk to my amigos. . . .'

I looked round and saw Trail and Archer disappearing up the stairs leading to the operational portion of the building.

'Hey!' I called, jumping up. 'Don't you fellows leave me!'

'It's all right, Doc. We won't be long.' Trail called over his shoulder. 'Finish the beer for us.'

I sat down gloomily and bit my lip, feeling like a warning to young men. The girl, discouraged, got up and left me. I took my handkerchief out and wiped my forehead.

But Madame, ever solicitous, assumed immediately that my companion had for some reason not pleased me. She directed a large grinning blonde to take her place.

'No, no!' I said in alarm. 'No! Please . . . go away, there's a good girl.'

'Não?'

'No. Sorry and all that.'

I looked uncomfortably round me. I wanted to get out. But I didn't know the way back to the ship, and I was scared to walk out of the place on my own. I took a gulp of beer and sat biting my thumbnail.

I was hardly aware that another had joined me. She sat quietly beside me without speaking. I looked up. She was sitting demurely with her hands clasped in her lap, as pathetic as a wallflower at a village dance.

'Hop it! Vamos! Pronto!' I told her.

'Please . . . please!' she said.

'My dear young lady, I have no intention . . .'

Two tears rolled compellingly down her thin cheeks.

'Please come,' she urged softly. 'No one come with me this week. If you no come I get fired.'

I licked my lips. This was the sort of dilemma even Big White Carstairs would have had difficulty sorting out.

She laid a hand on my arm, as softly as an alighting butterfly.

'Please come,' she whispered.

I coughed, and ran my finger round my collar. My conscience strained to suppress my sense of gallantry. Just then two large tears followed the first.

'How much?' I heard. It was me.

'Hun'red cruzeiro.'

'Oh . . . ah . . . very well then . . .'

I pulled the note from my pocket. Seizing it, she pulled me by the hand towards the staircase of sin.

We went into a bare room that contained only a bed, a basin, and several more pictures of the saints. She locked the door. I stood and scratched my left ear.

Deftly, as though peeling a banana, she stripped off her clothes. She jumped on the bed and gave me an inviting smile. Suddenly she held her right side and groaned.

'Hello,' I said, immediately interested. 'What's the trouble?'

She bit her lip for a moment, then said, 'Nada . . . nada.'

'Have you got a pain? Er—dor?'

She nodded.

'Where?'

She pointed under her right ribs.

'That's curious,' I said. 'Just let me have a look a minute, will you? By Jove, this is unusual . . . Deep breath, now.'

After five minutes' careful examination of her abdomen I concluded that the young lady was suffering from inflammation of the gall-bladder.

'Look here,' I said, 'you ought to go to hospital.'

She smiled up at me from the pillow.

'Hospital . . . operaçao, or whatever it is.'

I indicated with signs.

'Oh, não,' she said.

'Oh, yes,' I said firmly. 'Here'—I took a pencil and paper from my pocket and wrote on it—'you take that to the chemist—farmacêutico—and they'll give you something to make it better. Then you must go to hospital, see? O.K.?'

She took the prescription and grinned.

'Very well,' I said automatically, 'call me if you have any severe pain during the night. Good evening.'

I let myself out. Trail and Archer were waiting downstairs.

'Come on, you dirty old man,' Trail said, grabbing my arm. 'Time to get back to the ship.'

It occurred to me that was the only consultation I had ever paid for.

11

THE next morning I woke, sweating and penitent, in my unventilated cabin. Jumbled harbour sounds replaced our usual noiseless morning at sea, and the steam winches were already working in frantic bursts on the deck outside. There were footsteps and shouting all over the ship, and when I turned over for my watch I saw an unknown, half-naked Brazilian picking his teeth and solemnly inspecting me from the open cabin door. As I shaved I reflected sharply on the change in my recreations in the last four weeks.

At breakfast I found Archer and Trail as unruffled as if they had spent the evening in a suburban cinema.

'I hear you had a bit of a lash-up last night,' Hornbeam said. 'Have a good time in Mimi's?'

'One must see how the other half lives,' I murmured.

'She was a nice little piece you got hold of,' Trail said, in a complimentary tone. 'Wouldn't have minded her myself.'

Hornbeam, who had an unphysiological resilience to alcohol, nodded as he ate his way with relish through a dish of bacon, chops, eggs, and liver.

'Sorry I couldn't come with you blokes,' he said cheerfully. 'I reckon I was tired. The quartermaster put me in my bunk about three.'

'This is not much of a place, anyway,' Trail said. 'Not a patch on B.A.'

'They've cleaned up B.A. a lot now,' Archer added, with disappointment. 'Do you remember Underneath the Arches, Mr. Hornbeam? A string of them running down behind a sort of colonnade affair from the Boca practically to the Plaza de Majo. They had a purity campaign down there after the war.'

'They needed it,' Hornbeam said, reaching for the tomato sauce. 'Any more bacon going, steward? I get peckish in port.'

'What are you doing to-day, Doc?' Archer asked. 'Going ashore?'

'I was thinking of it.'

'What, going back for an encore?' Trail said.

'No, I assure you I was only thinking of a haircut.'

'You're right there, Doc,' Hornbeam said. 'You look like an old rope fender.'

My hair had last been cut in the wintery twilight of a London afternoon, more than a month ago: now it overhung my newly sunburned ears, and its length reflected our distance from home. But I was reluctant to step ashore alone, for the only Portuguese I was confident of saying was 'Good morning,' and I was not in the position to refuse a shampoo, singeing, scalp massage, hot towels, and any unusual luxuries that might be provided by Brazilian barber's shops. I explained this to Easter during surgery, and he immediately relieved my difficulties.

'I should be very glad to oblige, Doctor,' he said with dignity. 'If requested.'

'You cut hair, too, do you?'

'Done quite a few hair-cutting jobs ashore. Worked six months steady at it once, helping out a pal what had a little barber's shop in Doncaster. He ran a book really, but the shop kept the coppers away. Got pinched last year, so I heard.'

'Very well, Easter. You may try your skill on me.'

He set up his saloon on the strip of deck outside my cabin. He first spread out several sheets of the *Liverpool Echo*, then brought from his quarters a camp stool and a length of cloth striped like a butcher's apron. He tied the cloth tightly round my neck and drew a pair of scissors and a comb from his hip pocket.

'How do you like it?' he demanded.

'Oh, sort of short round the back.'

'Wouldn't like a crew cut, would you? Suit your sort of head, if I may be so bold, Doctor.'

'No, thank you.'

He began snipping round the nape of the neck.

'Bit of fun and games about noon,' he continued. 'The *Violet's* coming in astern of us where that Royal Mail boat was yesterday.'

'The *Violet?* What's she?'

'Another one of the Fathom hookers. Does the run from the River Plate to Pernambuco and New York. Captain Beamish in command. Cor! He ain't 'arf a queer 'un. Needs his head examined, I reckon.'

'That's what they're cleaning up the wheelhouse for, is it?'

'Ho yes, got to have her looking posh when we has company. Sorry, Doctor, was that your ear?'

'If I get a septic wound from this,' I said sternly, 'I shall order your kit to be burned as a sanitary measure.'

He blew hard through the comb and bit deeply into my hair with it.

'I likes hair-cutting,' he continued, unruffled. 'Bit of an art, like knocking up a sculpture. You never know how it's going to turn out when you start.'

I sat in the sunshine, unresisting, while my hair fell in small bundles across the *Liverpool Echo*. The increasing warmth and Easter's conversation behind the regular sharp snip of his scissors encouraged a pleasant feeling of euphoria. I was looking forrard, towards the mouth of the river; the long quay, with the tall German cranes grouped eagerly round open hatchways, was lined with ships as far as I could see. In the water on our port side a clean, grey-and-white, neat Swedish tanker was being turned slowly by a pair of tugs, like a birch log between two water-rats. Immediately ahead of us the Stars and Stripes dropped over the stern of the *Omar C. Ingersoll* of Baltimore, a cargo ship the same size as the *Lotus*, designed with the American combination of stark lines and grotesque, mysterious appendages. Just below me, on the foredeck, a dozen Brazilians clutched a swaying crate labelled AUSTIN that hovered from the sling over No. 2 hatch.

'I reckon you was right not to trust the barbers ashore,' Easter said. 'They ain't up to much, and they'll rook you as soon as look at you. Not as bad as the ones in Port Said, though—for a dollar they'll give you a shampoo and introduce you to their sister.' He wiped the comb on the leg of his trousers thoughtfully. 'Mind you,' he went on, 'you can have some fun in Port Said if you're up to the tricks. Very rude in places, it is, very rude.' He swept away the cloth and stood back proudly. 'Lovely,' he said. 'Care for me to read your bumps while I'm at it? Used to be Phreno the Bump Man at fairs for a bit.'

'That will be enough, thank you. How much do I owe you?'

'Fifty Woods, Doctor, seeing it's you.'

I went to my cabin to fetch the cigarettes, and found I looked like a caricature of a Prussian general; I suspected that Easter had learned the elements of barbering while serving one of his terms in jail. The advent of the *Violet* seemed to justify the Company's Regulation Cap, so I fitted a new white cover and stepped back on deck with Easter's art hidden underneath.

By now there was an atmosphere of serious preparation on board. Captain Hogg was shouting at a pair of deck-hands painting the large red F on the funnel, Hornbeam was supervising the desperate removal of a potful of black paint just spilled over the white bridge, and the Bos'n was trying to rig a line of electric bulbs along the gangway without disturbing the fat policeman who slept in a deckchair by the rail. As noon approached, the crew began leaning over the port rail and Captain Hogg climbed on the monkey island over the wheelhouse and impatiently trained his glasses towards the bow. I went to the boatdeck and squeezed between two davits, trying to catch the familiar Fathom Line houseflag moving slowly through the forest of strange masts.

'Mind you don't fall in,' Hornbeam said, coming up the ladder. 'A mouthful of this water would kill you. Any sign of her yet?'

'Can't see anything from here.'

'The Old Man and Beamish are great pals,' he told me contentedly. 'They'd ram each other's ships if they thought they could get away with it. Not that I have any time for Beamish,' he added. 'In fact, I'm not certain I wouldn't rather sail with the one we've got.'

E

This struck me as severely damning to Captain Beamish. 'What's the matter with him?'

'Thinks he's one of the big ship boys—you know, everything frightfully pukka, wipe your feet at the top of the gangway, kiss me hand and call me Charlie. They say he was a cadet in the P. & O., but got chucked out. I can't say I blame them.'

'But surely,' I said despairingly, 'there must be some good captains in the world?'

'There's one or two. Old Morris on the *Daisy* isn't bad. He did me a good turn once in Belfast when I got mixed up with the cops. But as soon as they get their fourth ring most of 'em get bloody-minded. You wait and see— I'll go the same way.'

We stood chatting between the lifeboats for a while, until Captain Hogg bellowed from above us: 'Ahoy there, Mr. Trail! Stand by to dip ensign!'

'There she is,' Hornbeam said, pointing down the river. 'See?'

'What, that?'

His account of Captain Beamish made me imagine his ship as equally superior; but the *Violet*, as she swung round the bend in the river, turned out to be a vessel smaller than the *Lotus*, narrow, as angular as a piano, with patches on her plates and two tall, mournful ventilators drooping over her bridge. She was high in the water, with a wide streak of red showing at the bottom of her rusty hull, and the tips of her propeller blades cut the surface below her overhanging stern.

'Makes us look like the *Queen Lizzie*, doesn't it?' Hornbeam said as she drew nearer. 'Watch for the fun when we start saluting.'

It was clear that Captain Hogg was going to pay his

respects grudgingly. He stood on top of the wheelhouse
glaring across the water to the *Violet,* and on the wing of
the *Violet's* bridge a thin, tall figure in a shining white
uniform glared back at him. As the mainmasts of the two
ships drew level Captain Hogg shouted 'Lower away!'
and the *Violet's* ensign fluttered down a foot in curt
acknowledgment. The two Captains scowled at each other
as they passed, and no one in either crew would have been
surprised if they had stuck out their tongues.

'The brotherhood of the sea,' Hornbeam said. 'I bet
Father's just waiting for her to foul our ropes as she comes
alongside.'

Captain Beamish nevertheless arrived for lunch on
board the *Lotus* as soon as his gangway was down. He
turned out to be a thin, brown, wrinkled man with a face
like a tortoise. He compensated for his own shabby ship
by turning himself out sprucely; his long neck stretched
from the high, starched collar of his uniform, two rows of
glossy medal ribbons shone on his bosom, his trousers were
unsullied with sitting, and his feet stood in white buckskin
shoes. He sat down at the table, placed a monocle in his
right eye, and crumbled a roll in his bony hand with an
expression on his face as if he expected it to release an
unpleasant smell.

Captain Hogg was coldly polite, and introduced us all.
'This is my Chief Officer, Mr. Hornbeam ... my Doctor ...
my Chief Engineer . . . my Chief Steward.' Captain
Beamish received these presentations in silence. Before we
had finished the soup it appeared that he was a man
sparing of words, for the only conversation he permitted
himself was to interrupt his host's remarks every few
minutes with the expression ' 'Strordinary!'

When we reached the treacle roll he cut into Captain

Hogg's description of how he once docked in Liverpool without tugs, by glaring at me and snapping, 'Doctor!'

'Sir?'

'Which hospital d'y' come from?'

'St. Swithin's, sir.'

'Strordinary! Must know Dr. Jenkins.'

'Jenkins? No, I'm afraid I don't, sir.'

'Jenkins was a very well-known man in the Line.'

I shook my head solemnly, without making any comment. I had gathered that doctors became well known in seafaring life only through the originality with which they left it.

'You look very young, Doctor,' he continued. 'Fully qualified, I suppose?'

'Of course I am!' I said angrily.

' 'Strordinary. Looks very young indeed,' he added in a slightly softer voice to Captain Hogg, who immediately began looking at me with suspicion.

'Lost my damned Bos'n this trip,' Captain Beamish went on. 'Blast him.'

'What was up?' Captain Hogg asked, piling the last fragments of suet roll on to his spoon.

'Had to put him over the wall off Pernam. Dead, y'know.'

'Go on! What of?'

' 'Strordinary thing altogether. Meant to ask your Doctor. Had a turn of the shakes and died before sunset.'

'Very likely smallpox,' I said firmly. 'Your ship will have to be fumigated for three weeks and all hands isolated in the fever hospital. The one in Santos is extremely unpleasant, but they will probably take you up to São Paulo as you're certain to get it, anyway.'

I sat and sulked over the cheese-dish.

'Bad about the Bos'n,' Captain Beamish said. 'Don't get his type any more. Respectful. Knew my ways. I may not be in command of a big ship, but I'll have her run decently. Eh, Captain?'

Captain Hogg had his mouth full of cheese, but he nodded violently enough to spill pieces on to the table-cloth.

'Don't know what things are coming to. The Third wore the same uniform three days running last week. D'y'know what happened yesterday? Steward brought me a glass of water without a tray. Communism, that's what it is.'

Captain Beamish then said nothing else for the rest of the meal.

The *Violet's* officers came aboard before supper and noisily packed themselves into Hornbeam's cabin. I found it startling to see the familiar Fathom Line uniforms and badges with different faces over them. They sat and drank gin, enjoying the fragmentary friendship of the sea that had been established by a few hours or a day or two in a dozen years at ports all over the world.

'Here's our Doc,' Hornbeam said, as I squeezed through the door. 'Meet Mr. Molony, Chief Officer from that old barge down aft.'

'Hello, Doc,' he said, shaking hands. 'Enjoying the sea?'

'I am, rather, thank you.'

'How did you get on with our Old Man at dinner?'

'I must say he was pretty rude.'

Molony laughed loudly, while Hornbeam filled up his glass.

'He takes some getting used to. Do you know what?' he asked Hornbeam. 'He chased me up for eating peas off a knife the other day. Can you imagine it? Now there's bugling, too. We signed on a Yankee galley-boy in New

York who brought a trumpet with him, so we get bugle calls to meals. Anyone would think we were a ruddy battleship.'

'All skippers are the same,' Hornbeam said wearily. 'Do you remember old Jack Andrews in the *Buttercup?* What happened to him?'

'Didn't you hear? He got put ashore in Cape Town last year.'

They began to talk earnestly of men and ships I had never heard of, and their conversation took on an odd parochialism extending across the face of the earth.

As the *Violet* was due to sail again at midnight our guests left early. I leant on the rail and watched her float slowly into the river, her portholes drawing yellow streaks across the greasy water. She blew three hoots of farewell to us and followed her tug towards the sea. Captain Hogg stood outside his cabin staring after her, and no doubt Captain Beamish was on the bridge glaring astern at us. I wondered if I should meet any more Fathom Line captains, and if they would be any less unnerving.

A man in a pair of khaki trousers and a loose orange shirt was waiting in my cabin. He grinned as I came in.

'Hi'ya, Doc,' he said. 'I'm off the *Omar C. Ingersoll.* Pleased to meet ya.'

We shook hands.

'I guess I shouldn't have bust in, but your Chief Mate said it was O.K.'

'Perfectly all right,' I said. 'What can I do for you?'

'I just want a bottle of aspirin. We're right out, and we ain't carrying a medic. I don't want to put you to no bother, though.'

'No trouble at all, my good man,' I said. 'I'll fetch you some from the hospital.'

'That's mighty swell of you, Doc,' he said, grinning at me again. 'Mighty swell.'

In return for the bottle of aspirins he presented me with two hundred Chesterfields, *The Case of the Luckless Legs*, three bars of chocolate, *Life*, and a photograph of the *Omar C. Ingersoll*. At the gangway he slapped me on the back and said, 'Come aboard and have a cup of coffee sometime, Doc. Just go up the gangway and ask for me.'

'Very kind of you,' I said. 'And you are . . . the Bos'n? Er, Mate, possibly . . .?'

'Aw, hell no, Doc! I'm the Captain. So long!'

I went to my bunk reflecting that the feudal system at least had the advantage of leaving you in no doubt whom you were talking to.

12

WE spent a week in Santos, all baking in our cabins like a big dish of *escargots*. Our next port was to be Buenos Aires, to load grain and hides for home.

'Shan't be sorry to get away,' said Trail the morning we sailed. 'Stinking place, this. Fancy living here!'

'When are we off?'

'About midday. They've finished cargo in all hatches except No. 5. It's hot, isn't it? I'll be like a fried egg when I come off the bridge.'

We left the city of tolerance behind us and turned south towards the River Plate.

Our voyage down the coast was enlivened by Christmas, which fell upon us half-way between Santos and Montevideo. The festival is celebrated most warmly by Englishmen when away from their own country, just as London Scots afford the fiercest welcome to the New Year. As I had now a fair insight into the behaviour of the *Lotus* and her crew I expected the day would pass with a flourish.

On Christmas morning Easter awoke me with my tea at seven.

'Good morning, Doctor. And a Merry Christmas to you, Doctor, with my best respects.'

'Thank you, Easter. And the same to you.'

'Bloody 'ot again, ain't it?'

'What's on the thermometer?'

He looked at it closely.

'Hundred and two. Won't be nearly so chilly by mid-day, neither.'

'It seems very strange to me to have Christmas in this climate.'

'Cor,' Easter continued, 'I remember one Christmas we had in the Timor Sea. I was in a Yankee ship then—one of them all-metal jobs inside. She was hot enough to melt a bos'n's heart. Early on Christmas morning the Chief Engineer goes and dies, see . . .'

'Really, Easter . . .'

'. . . so I reckons we got to chuck the poor bastard over the wall pronto, because in that heat you wouldn't be able to get near him after dinner-time, let alone dress him up in a canvas suit. I tells the Mate—nasty bit of work he was—but he won't have none of it. You know what these Yanks are. Crazy for embalming. "He's got to be embalmed," he says, "then we'll pop him in the galley freezer and he can have a decent burial in the soil of God's Own Country. Besides," he says, "we ain't going to have no funerals on Christmas Day." "Yes," I says, "but who's going to do the embalming?" "You are," he says, "there's instructions in the Pharmacist's Mate's Hand-book, and you can get on with it. If you do him nice I'll give you a bottle of Scotch, and if you makes a pig's bottom of him I'll kick you round the deck."

'What could I do? I tells the Skipper, but he gets a cob on and says it's orders. So I reckon instead of arguing it's best to get on with it while he's still pretty fresh. The Butcher and me goes in there and gets to work, me promising the Butch half of the Scotch—used to be in the meat works at Chicago, the Butch, and reckoned something like that was right up his alley.

'Oh, we made a lovely job of him,' Easter continued with pride. 'It would have brought tears to his mother's eyes. When we'd finished the Butch and I gets the hospital stretcher to carry him down to the freezer, while the Skipper and all hands gathers round the cabin door to have a dekko. I goes in first holding one end of the stretcher, the Butch holding the other, and the Mate comes in after us to see what sort of a job we've made of him. Well, I dunno. Either we'd made the poor bloke so lifelike, or it was that hot, or he was starting to pong a bit, but the Mate gets inside and passes out like a light. So what could we do? The Butch and I puts him on the stretcher and carries him on deck for some air. When the Skipper sees us coming out with the Mate lying there instead of the corpse he takes one look and bloody well faints as well. Cor, what a lash-up! Stiffs all over the deck. Wasn't 'arf a funny Christmas, that wasn't.'

'Thank you, Easter,' I said. 'You have cheered my Christmas morn.'

'The Bos'n's got toothache,' he added.

'Has he? How badly?'

'Something cruel, he reckons.'

'Send him to the hospital. I'll be along in half an hour.'

The bos'n was a big man with a complexion like an old football and a face as threatening as a battleship's gun-turret. I found him sitting in the hospital chair, holding his jaw and moaning.

'Merry Christmas,' I said.

I shone a torch in his mouth and announced 'It'll have to come out.'

'O.K., Doc,' he said, squaring his shoulders. 'I can take it.'

We had fortunately found a pair of dental forceps on board, and I hoped they would fit the tooth. I had never extracted one before, but from the ranks of dentists I had seen in action in the hospital out-patient department it looked pretty simple. One simply pulled hard, as though extracting a nail from a plank, and the tooth appeared in a flurry of saliva and blood.

'Easter,' I said. 'What have we in the way of anæsthetics?'

'If I may be so bold, sir, and especially seeing it's Christmas, how about the medical comforts?'

'Capital idea. Are there any left?'

'I took the liberty of telling the Chief Steward last night that you was wanting some special for the season.'

'Very well. Go and fetch them, Easter.'

The three of us sat in a circle and purposefully drank brandy.

'Have another glass,' I told the Bos'n. 'After all, you're the patient.'

He said the pain was beginning to wear off.

'Nevertheless,' I said firmly, 'we must proceed with the operation. I don't want you messing up my Christmas Day with toothache. Open wide,' I commanded. I applied the forceps. 'Is that the one?'

He nodded vigorously.

I gripped the forceps hard and pulled. It was like trying to crack a fresh Brazil nut. I gave another tug. The Bos'n grunted and screwed his eyes up.

'This may hurt a little,' I remembered to say.

I threw all my weight against the tooth. Sweat was running down my face and into my eyes and I was breathing like a middle-aged wrestler.

'It's no good!' I grunted. 'I'm just not tough enough. Easter, apply counter-pressure to his shoulders, will you? That's right. Now—one, two, three, together heave!'

The patient slipped down the chair.

'Oh Lord!' I said.

'If I might suggest,' Easter said. 'Dr. Flowerday used to find it very useful to put his knee in the bloke's chest.'

'Like that?'

'That's right, Doctor. Now shove your elbows against his shoulders.'

There was a crash, and the patient landed on the deck with me on top of him.

'Hold on, Doctor!' Easter shouted. 'It's coming!'

I set my jaw and threw myself into a final effort; but the tooth was as firm as a rivet in a ship's plate. I was about to roll off the patient in exhaustion when he decided it was time to intervene himself. Two large, powerful hands came up and enveloped mine. The Bos'n gave a sharp heave and the tooth came out like a pip from an orange.

He stood up, spat a mouthful of blood in the sink and looked at me anxiously.

'Are you all right, Doctor?' he asked. 'Didn't hurt you, did I?'

'No, I think I'm all right,' I panted.

'Gawd, that's better! Merry Christmas, Doctor.'

The Bos'n walked contentedly aft, and I went to join my shipmates. There was an air of geniality on board, fostered not only by the season but the fact that Christmas was technically Sunday and therefore everyone had another half-day's pay.

After midday the officers were invited to Captain Hogg's cabin for drinks. Everyone came—even the Chief Engineer, who allowed his aversion for both the Captain and the foolish Sassenach custom of celebrating on December 25th to be overcome by his satisfaction of getting a free drink out of his enemy.

The Captain had already been setting himself in the mood for Christmas, and welcomed us with guarded geniality. We were all cleanly dressed and sober, except the Wireless Operator, who had already been having a party in his cabin with his own friends.

'Good morning, gentlemen, good morning!' Captain Hogg said, giving us a cold smile. 'Compliments of the season, gentlemen, on behalf of myself and the Company.'

'It was Christmas Day in the workhouse . . .' the Sparks began. Hornbeam clapped a hand over his mouth.

'Help me with the drinks, Mr. Whimble, will you? That's right. Pink gins all round, I suppose? Help yourselves to iced water, gentlemen. Here's to a Merry Christmas.'

'Same to you, sir!' everyone said, respectfully raising their glasses.

'. . . the Master called down the halls,' the Sparks continued. 'Did you like your Christmas dinner? And the inmates answered . . .'

Hornbeam shut him up again.

'I propose,' Captain Hogg said, glancing sternly round the company, 'on this solemn day in our year to make a short speech.'

There were murmurs of assent all round: he had as much risk of objection as Hitler ever had.

'This is *my* ship,' Captain Hogg went on. 'My ship. She is in my care, and so are the lives of all of you in her.' He took a swallow of gin. 'My ambition,' he continued, 'is to have a happy ship. Do you understand? That means that every damn one of you's got to knuckle under. This ship—my ship'—he waved his glass expansively—'is a floating village. We have our butcher, our baker, and our lamptrimmer. We have our own storekeeper—even our own doctor.' This brought a roar of laughter and a round of applause. 'But I'—he hit his chest—'I am the squire of the village. Get that straight. Give me another gin, Mr. Whimble.'

'On this occasion,' he resumed, 'I look upon you all with a fatherly eye. All of you. I am proud of you. You are the best crew I've ever sailed with. You are——'

He stopped. He glared out of the porthole. His face twisted alarmingly. The *Lotus* had stopped.

'Mr. McDougall,' he hissed, 'the ship's stopped.'

McDougall didn't move.

'Aye,' he said.

'What is it?' Captain Hogg asked heavily. 'Are you celebrating Christmas so much down below that you have let the boilers go out?'

McDougall carefully drained his gin.

'We no celebrate these cissy festivals in my department. We save it up for Hogmanay.'

'So! You come up here and take my liquor——'

'And listen to an old windbag like you——'

'How dare you, sir! I have never been insulted like that in all my years at sea!'

'All your years! I was on watch below when you were flying yellow at the mizzen.'

Captain Hogg shook a fist at him.

'I was in sail, sir!'

'You ought to have stayed there. You'd make a good barge skipper.'

'We didn't need engineers in those days,' Captain Hogg shouted.

'And in ten years' time we won't need captains.'

'Damn you, sir! I won't be talked to like this! I'll have you logged. I will. I mean it. I——'

'It was Christmas Day in the workhouse——' the Sparks began.

'Aw, go to hell!' McDougall said.

'Please, please!' cried Whimble.

'I've had enough of this, Mr. McDougall——!'

'And I've had more than enough——!'

'Steady the Buffs!' said Hornbeam jovially.

At that moment the Second Steward arrived and announced that dinner was served.

The saloon was decorated with dusty streamers that were produced every year, like the dinner menu, irrespective of the latitude in which the *Lotus* found herself. The English are the greatest colonizing race in the world, but they show a reluctance to part with their native habits in climates that render them highly unsuitable or even unhealthy. Wherever two Englishmen are together at Christmas the accustomed dinner must be eaten, in its full carbohydrate glory. The weather demanded a little salad and an ice cream, but we sat down and dutifully faced the full gastronomic trappings of the season—roast turkey, sausages, cold pork, roast beef, boiled cabbage, roast potatoes, mince pies, and Christmas pudding.

'We've got a nice veal and ham pie on as well, if you want any,' Whimble whispered in my ear as we went in.

All the officers off watch were crammed round the saloon table. Captain Hogg sat at the head, with McDougall opposite him. The *Lotus* shivered and started again, and they glared at each other over the tomato soup.

Free whisky was given to all hands, and Whimble handed each officer a paper hat, with a plea not to crush it as they would have to make do for the following year.

I was cutting my first slice of turkey when Hornbeam, who was next to me, gave a nudge.

'Your man seems to want you,' he said.

Easter was standing sheepishly in the doorway.

I excused myself to Captain Hogg and went over to him.

'What is it?' I asked.

'Having a nice dinner, Doctor?'

'Well, if that's all you came to say . . .'

'There's been trouble in the poop.'

'Trouble? What sort of trouble?'

'Couple of the lads has been fighting.'

'Oh, all right. Who are they?'

'Two of the stewards. Myrtle and Mavis.'

'Who did you say?'

Easter grinned. 'You'll find out,' he said.

Two tall, silky-haired young men who cleaned the cabins were sitting in the hospital. They were both covered in blood, and one was in tears.

'What the devil's been going on?' I asked the other.

His lip quivered and he, too, began to weep.

'Another little problem of the sea,' Easter remarked tolerantly. 'Them blokes as is a bit late making up their minds whether they're men or women.'

'Oh lord!' I said. 'What were they fighting about?'

'I didn't do it!' the first one cried. 'I swear on my honour I didn't!'

'Oh, yes you did!' the other shouted. 'You give it back at once, you mean thing!'

'How can I give it back if I haven't got it?'

'Yes you have! You've been trying to sneak it all the voyage!'

'I haven't got that beastly lipstick! It isn't my colour, anyway.'

They started pulling each other's hair.

'They're a bit queer,' Easter explained helpfully.

'Well, do something about them, man! Pour water on them! Get the Mate, and I'll have them logged.'

Easter hit one over the head with an arm-splint.

'Turn it up,' he said genially. 'It's Christmas.'

I put dressings on the unfortunate couple and went back to dinner. By that time everything had been eaten and Captain Hogg was on his feet again, making another speech.

'. . . I have said before,' he told the company, leaning on the table, 'and I say it again—I am proud of my crew. The crew of *my* ship. I shall put in my report to the Company that you are the best crew——'

His face clouded over. He snarled. The *Lotus* had stopped again.

13

THE rest of the day passed unalarmingly. We were nearing the busy coast of Uruguay, where the River Plate shipping first turns north to Europe and the States. That night I stood on the hot deck in my pyjamas and watched the quiet sea swishing unhurriedly past the *Lotus*'s side. Another ship approached us, two broken rows of lights in the darkness, her green starboard light shining into ours. An Aldis light flashed from her bridge, calling us up. I watched the Third Mate reply. I supposed we only wished each other a Merry Christmas and exchanged the usual courtesy queries about name and destination, but it made me realize for the first time that the *Lotus* was not the only ship on the sea: all over the world there were tiny floating communities, with the same sort of people doing the same sort of things as we did—keeping parallel watches, eating similar meals, listening to the identical strokes of another ship's bell. There were other doctors, other mates, other captains, each ship struggling with its own apparently paramount problems. I yawned, as Captain Hogg shrank into comforting perspective.

When I went to turn in I found Hornbeam in my cabin.

'Hello, Doc. Just dropped in for a final peg, seeing it's Christmas night. Do you mind?'

'Not a bit. Help yourself to the Scotch.'

'Thanks.'

He put his feet up on the desk.

'Father made a fine showing to-day,' he said.

'Where is he now?'

'Sleeping it off. I just went up to see if the Third Mate's sober. You've never seen any of us go on watch sloshed, have you?'

'No, never.'

'It doesn't matter about the Old Man. Some of 'em kill a bottle a day and still keep their jobs.' He stretched. 'I wish this one would drop dead,' he said amiably.

'You'd get promotion, you mean?'

He nodded.

'I'm next on the list. Trouble is, all the other skippers in the Company are as healthy as apprentices. They'll have to give me a command soon,' he added, sadly. 'I'm getting too old and fat to go running up and down hatch ladders.'

'You'll get one soon enough.'

'I don't know. All I want is a command—it doesn't matter if the ship sinks as soon as we get out of port. As long as I can call myself Captain. That's what I've been at sea for all these years—all the way up, apprentice, third, second, mate. That's what keeps us sane, most of us. Waiting for a ship of our own. Then I'm going to chuck the sea and raise chickens.'

'I bet you won't.'

'It's a mug's game. When you've been at it a couple of

years they've got you where they want you. There's nothing for you ashore—what good's a master's ticket in the Labour Exchange? The sea's a positive bitch. You can't run away from her if you want to.'

'I suppose you're right there.'

'You staying at sea, Doc?'

'Me? Oh, no. I'm going back to general practice in the provinces, I suppose.' I saw the grey streets, the grey skies, the grey complexions of the patients; wet winter mornings and acrid summer ones; frightened faces on the doorstep at three in the morning; four o'clock parties with conversation like the weak over-sweetened tea; hedging respectability, the eternal narrowness of the persistent provincial.

'Perhaps,' I added.

'Well,' Hornbeam said. 'The only thing to do with life is to live it, you know. Shall we have a last one?' I passed him the bottle. 'We'll be in B.A. to-morrow,' he added more cheerfully. 'You can have some fun there.'

*　　*　　*　　*

'Everything's on the top line here since they had the purity campaign,' the Third said. 'Now it's as clean as Blackpool. Pity.'

We were lying off the big, white, flat city of Buenos Aires, lines of tall, angular buildings running down to the clean waterfront.

'It's pretty nice here in the New Port,' the Third went on.

'Where do we go?' I asked.

'Down by the meat works.'

Two hours later the *Lotus* was coaxed through the narrow entrance of the South Dock, and tied up not far from the big grey refrigerating plant.

'Smells like a farm, don't it?' Easter remarked, as we were drawing alongside. 'Don't 'arf get a lot of flies down here. Thick as coppers on a racecourse, they are.'

'So this is where the beef comes from?'

'That's it. They walk in one end and half an hour later they slides out in a tin. Smart, these boys are.'

Our reception was the same as in Santos, except that everyone spoke Spanish. The same functionaries hurried aboard, made for the Mate's cabin, and drank the Mate's gin, from which the business of the ship seemed inseparable. But Hornbeam was determined, for once, to go ashore.

'I've only had a couple all day,' he said proudly to me. 'Look at the bottle for yourself. I'm going to take you lads on a treat to-night. See you about ten.'

'I'll hold you to that.'

'Word of honour, Doc.'

Hornbeam kept his promise. When Trail, Archer, and myself met him in his cabin he was glowing but not extinguished.

'Just a quick one before we leave,' he said, unclipping the cap of another gin bottle. 'It's all on me to-night, boys. I've got plenty of pesos.'

'Where did you land them from?' Archer asked.

Hornbeam winked.

'The Mate's got to have a few perks,' he explained. 'Small present from the stevedores for giving them the pleasure of our custom. Also a token from the chandlers for the honour of providing us with deck stores. Strictly against Company regs., of course. Oh, I've got about'— he pulled some notes from his pocket—'about a thousand pesos.'

'That's forty quid,' Trail said reverently.

'Nothing but the best to-night!' Hornbeam continued. 'Drink up, and we'll hit the town.'

'This is the Boca,' Hornbeam explained, as we walked over the railway tracks towards the gawky German gantry bridge. 'One of the toughest spots in South America. A bos'n I sailed with once got beaten up about here. Left him only his shoes. He was a big chap, too.'

'I wish they wouldn't put ships in such insalubrious districts,' I said. 'It's like living in the slums.'

'They reckon the slums are good enough for sailors, I suppose.'

To reach the town we climbed into a small boat and were rowed across the slimy river towards the Boca's main street.

'Hard work finding a taxi in B.A. these days,' Trail said. 'We'd better climb in a colectivo.'

'A quick one in old Mother Whitebread's first,' Archer insisted. 'After all, it's known to every Liverpool fireman since steam came in.'

We had a couple of drinks described guardedly as Special Cocktails, and ate bits of chopped meat, nuts, mussels, cheese, and olives from the small plates the citizens of Buenos Aires expect to be handed with their drinks.

'On me,' Hornbeam said firmly, pulling out a fifty-peso note. 'Now let's go down town and have a steak.'

We went to the broad, bright Avenida Corrientes, the Broadway of B.A. In one of the grill rooms we sat down and ate steaks three inches thick.

'Nothing like nourishment,' Hornbeam observed. 'I'm going to have another of these. How about you, Doc?'

I shook my head, as my mouth was too full to speak.

'You'll want it in a few weeks' time when you're

treating yourself to a nice spaghetti on toast. How about
a bottle of Argentine wine? It's not bad. All on me, you
blokes.'

We rose uneasily from the table when Hornbeam paid
the bill. By now his already generous feelings towards the
evening were accentuated by heavy feeding.

'I'm going to show you boys the town,' he said hand-
somely. 'Everything's my treat. Where shall we go to?'

'How about El Nidito?' Archer suggested. 'Or
L'Atelier?'

'There's a joint I used to know round the corner,'
Hornbeam said, scratching his forehead. 'Little redhead
in there plays the guitar.'

He was delighted to find the bar was still there, though,
reasonably enough, the redhead wasn't. It was a small, dim
place with a band playing sambas in the corner and a tall
girl caressing a microphone not much thinner than herself.

'Lovely grub!' Hornbeam said with relish. 'What's it
to be? Scotch?'

There was no Scotch but they gave us the locally
distilled whisky, which tasted like an old-fashioned
carminative mixture. Trail got into earnest conversation
with the girl behind the bar, who came from Lytham St.
Anne's, and I sat wondering what the whisky was doing
to my gastric lining.

'I've had this place,' Hornbeam said impatiently after
a few minutes. 'Let's move on.'

'But we've only just arrived.'

'It's too quiet. Come on, blokes. It's my party, so I
can take it anywhere.'

We went to a good many bars. They all offered the
same—darkness, sambas, local whisky, and a girl behind
the bar who came from some spot comparable to Lytham.

'It's half-past one,' I said to Archer later. 'Doesn't anyone go to sleep in B.A.?'

'Things are only beginning. They go on like this all night.'

'They must be a tougher race than we are. Apart from the hours, they seem to put up with their own whisky.'

Hornbeam was seized with a final inspiration.

'Let's go to the Saratoga, boys,' he announced.

'That's a posh do,' Trail told him dubiously. 'It's an expensive joint, particularly at this hour of the night.'

'Only the best is good enough for us,' Hornbeam insisted. 'Saratoga next stop. I want to see the dancing girls.'

We found a cab and drove down the street to the Saratoga. It was a class above the bars and night clubs we had been to—a small silk-lined place with two bands, a tiny dance floor, and a stage. Hornbeam strode in and demanded a table at the front.

'This is more like it!' he said contentedly. 'I'm fed up with slumming.'

He ordered some champagne.

I looked around me and saw it was certainly more fortunate in its clientele than the other places we had visited. The tone was marred only by our party, in which Hornbeam was now leaning back in his chair, clapping his hands, and demanding 'Bring on the fat women!'

'There aren't any here, are there?' I asked Archer.

'You wait, Doc,' he said. 'Three blokes can't sit down alone anywhere south of Panama without something turning up.'

He was right. A good-looking blonde in a white evening gown sat on the chair beside me.

'You buy me a t'rink, no?' she said.

The waiter had already appeared and brought her a thimbleful of red liquid in a liqueur glass. He also brought a green counter, which he handed to her. This she placed in her handbag.

'I'd better put you wise,' Archer said across the table. 'Out here you buy the coloured water and she gets the commission. If you can last out till four you go home with her buckshee.'

'I don't think I can last out the next ten minutes.'

The girl swallowed her glassful swiftly, like a bad medicine.

'You buy me another t'rink, no?'

The waiter gave her a second glass, and another counter.

'This is going to work out expensive,' I said.

'All on me, Doc,' Hornbeam said grandly. 'Tell her to send her friends over.'

Two more girls appeared and started drinking with the frightening rapidity of their companion. However, we all became very friendly, and Hornbeam ordered some more champagne.

When Trail fell asleep on the table I said, 'Hadn't we better get the bill, Chief? I could do with some sleep myself.'

'Mozo!' Hornbeam demanded. 'Bill, pronto!'

It was given to him immediately, neatly folded on a plate. He scowled at the figures, and began counting notes from his pocket.

'You buy me anot'er t'rink, no?' said the blonde.

'No. The bar's down.'

She got up and walked away.

'Say, Doc,' Hornbeam called. 'Can you lend me five hundred pesos?'

'What!'

'I seem to be a bit short.' Hornbeam spread his notes on the table. He had been carried away by his generosity into a ditch of insolvency.

We searched in our pockets, waking Trail up to join in.

'Ninety-eight pesos,' Archer said. 'That's all we can muster.'

Hornbeam looked shiftily over his shoulder. The waiter, with that second sight which waiters have, was aware that some hitch had arisen and threw dark glances at us. Visions of Argentine prisons shimmered before my eyes: I was sure the Buenos Aires police would arrest with the alacrity of their comrades in Santos.

'This is serious,' I said. 'Hasn't anyone got any money at all?'

We searched our pockets again.

'Not a centavo,' Trail said. 'I've got a couple of bob though.'

'Someone will have to go back to the ship and raise the wind,' Archer said. 'That's all there is for it. The others will sit here and pretend they're enjoying themselves. We'll toss for who goes.'

We tossed a twenty-centavo piece. I lost.

'Better take the ninety-eight pesos and see if you can get a cab,' Hornbeam said. 'Make it snappy. Ten pound notes will cover it at black-market rates.'

I stood outside in the hot dry air, already feeling the apprehending hand on my shoulder. I saw an empty cab on the other side of the street and leapt towards it.

'Dock Sul,' I said.

But the driver could take me only as far as the rowing boat. I had to cross the river and walk alone across the

railway tracks to the ship. I strode breathlessly along the
middle of the road, looking behind me more than in front.
A cat leapt across my path from shadow to shadow and I
yelped. I ran through the dock gates and up the gangway.

The *Lotus* was dead. The quartermaster was in a chair
by the gangway, asleep. Everyone not ashore was in their
bunks, wallowing in the deep unhindered unconsciousness
of watch-keepers in port.

I thought my best chance was represented by the Chief
Engineer. He was lying with his mouth open on top of
his bunk.

'Chief!' I called softly. I shook him. 'Chief!'

He stopped snoring and grunted.

'Chief! Wake up!'

He opened his eyes.

'Stop the feed pumps and stand-by all engineers,' he
said.

'No Chief! It's the Doc. Can you lend me some money?'

'Money? What for, man? At this hour of night.'

'I'll explain later. But I must have it now. In a hurry.'

'Wait till I put my teeth in, lad.'

He gave me five pound notes. The rest I collected by
rousing Whimble, the Second Steward, three or four of
the engineers, and Easter.

I ran back to the ferry, crumpling the notes in
my hands. I had to walk half a mile up the long road
to the City before I found a taxi. When I jumped out
I found my expedition had taken the best part of an hour,
and the Saratoga was rising to a final burst of activity
before closing for the night. I looked in nervously,
wondering if my companions had already been extracted
by the police, or had generously been allowed to wash
dishes in the basement.

Neither of these misfortunes had occurred to them. In my absence they had all drawn a second wind and were enjoying themselves hugely. They had three new girls and another bottle of champagne.

'I've got the money,' I said breathlessly, falling into a chair.'

'Ah, there's the old Doc!' Hornbeam said with surprise. 'Where did you come from?'

'I went to get some money to pay the bill,' I said angrily. 'Don't you remember.'

'That's right,' Archer agreed. 'Good old Doc. Mozo! Bill!'

Another bill was presented. Before they read the figures I knew what was coming.

'That ten quid means five hundred pesos,' Hornbeam said solemnly. 'Then there's this here—have you got any left, Doc?'

I threw him a few peso notes.

'Umm,' he said. 'Looks as if we need about five hundred pesos.'

'Well,' Trail said brightly. 'The Doc had better go back for some more.'

I banged the table.

'No!' I said. 'No, I damn well won't! I don't care if we all go to jail, but I'm not going back to the ship!'

The manager, who had been hovering in the distance like a well-preened vulture, put his head into our group.

'Anything wrong, gentlemen?' he asked.

'Yes,' I said. 'We can't pay the bill.'

I folded my arms and prepared to be arrested with the dignity of an Englishman.

'Unfortunate,' said the manager.

'Bloody unfortunate,' Hornbeam said.

'How much are you gentlemen short? Five hundred pesos, I see. You are seafaring gentlemen, are you not?'

'Don't we look like it?' I said.

'A not uncommon predicament. Always seafaring gentlemen. A nice watch you have,' he said to Trail. 'Must be worth at least a hundred pesos.'

'It cost me twenty quid in Durban,' Trail said hotly. I stopped him.

'Hand it over,' I said.

He sulkily unstrapped his watch.

'You other gentlemen have equally valuable time-pieces,' the manager continued.

'Your turn,' Trail said, brightening a little.

Hornbeam, Archer, and I surrendered ours.

'I think,' the manager continued, 'a Parker 51 would settle it.'

I gave him the pen from my pocket.

'Now get the hell out of here, you bums,' he said, 'or I'll get the cops on you.'

We stood, a forlorn quartet, on the pavement.

'Oh well,' said Hornbeam. 'You know what I told you the other night. The only thing to do with life is to live it. Now let's start walking back to the ship.'

14

IF you must be broke, there are many conveniences
in being broke as a seafarer on ship's articles. The
necessities of life, such as food, shelter, cigarettes, and
gin, continue to be supplied regularly, either free or on
account until the end of the voyage; and the state arouses
among one's companions a lively sympathy expressed on
land only on occasions of severe illness or other bitter
natural misfortune. When the story of our visit to the
Saratoga spread round the ship the next morning we
were chivvied with offers of help from all hands.

'Had a bit of a night of it, I hear, Doctor,' Easter said
jovially.

'I'm afraid so.'

'I don't hold with that there Saratoga,' he continued
reflectively. 'Mind you, they has some very posh tarts
there, very posh. But they don't 'arf burn up the rhino.
Is it worth it? I ask you. Now, me and Chippy goes ashore
quiet like, and has a few beers in old Ma Whitehead's.
If we feels like indulging, as you might say, we goes round
the back to a little place what Chippy reckons he was
first taken to by his father when he was sailing as a

deckboy. Mind, they ain't no great beauties in there. In fact, Chippy reckons they're the same ones what his father knew. But they come economic like, and that's something these days, ain't it, Doctor?'

'Thank you, Easter. I appreciate your little lecture on thrift.'

'We lives and learns, Doctor. How about a small contribution, if you've run yourself short?' He pulled a bundle of pesos notes from his jacket pocket.

'Definitely no!' I held up my hand, 'I insist on suffering justly for my indiscretions. Besides, I am already in debt to you. If you lent me any more you might not have enough left for your own modest pleasures, such as you have just described.'

'That's all right, Doctor. I just flogged some of that there penicillin what was expired. Dr. Flowerday and I used to split it fifty-fifty, but I don't mind taking forty-sixty to oblige. Barmy on penicillin, these Argentinos, I got rid of them there pills we didn't know what they was—them green ones in the back of the locker. Told 'em they was good for virility and charged a peso each. They go in for that sort of stuff a lot down here.'

'It is very kind of you, Easter, but—for reasons which I should be ashamed to confess—I much prefer you to keep the proceeds to yourself.'

'As you say, Doctor. Tip me the wink if you wants anything flogging. Wouldn't like a few tins of beef, would you? I scrounged some when a case bust going into No. 1 hold.'

'No thank you. But I appreciate your generosity. Just get me another pitcher of iced water from the galley.'

I put on my cap and went on deck. It was almost noon. The sun, as coarse and uninhibited as everything else in the region, shone savagely on the white planks and brown steel of the decks; but the river, the ships, and the quay were as peaceful as an English village on a high summer afternoon. The purring electric cranes were still and stood at untidy angles along the wharf with crates of merchandise at their feet, abandoned by the dockers for the midday break. Some of the stevedores lay asleep in the shade that was sharply cut out here and there by corners and eaves; others languidly masticated their lunch inside the doors of the airless sheds. From somewhere downstream came the subdued hoot of a small ship's whistle, and the regular soft thumping of some essential pump. The steers mooed spasmodically in the unseen corrals behind the meat works, and the flies, unaffected by the general langour, buzzed in thick, irritating squadrons everywhere.

I leaned on the hot rail and looked at the grey walls of the Frigorifico Anglo, which was temporarily inactive for lunch. I began to understand the disadvantages of my abrupt poverty: we should be in Buenos Aires for at least a fortnight, and the Frigorifico, though of superb interest as a commercial and technical undertaking and with appreciable merit as an example of functional design, would soon become oppressive as the largest segment of my daily horizon. I hadn't even the bus fare to the City.

While I was examining these bleak thoughts Trail came and leaned next to me. We discussed our condition in a few words.

'There's not much to be done here if you're broke,' he observed. 'We could rustle up enough to go to the pictures, I suppose.'

'I can do that in London.'

'That's true. They've got some nice parks, so they tell me.'

We had adjusted ourselves to a dull stay in one of the world's gayest capitals when a bright ray of entertainment abruptly shone into our lives from an unexpected source. I was lying on my bunk after dinner, reading the first paragraph of *War and Peace* with the drowsy inattentive righteousness of a good churchgoer sitting through a summer sermon, when Easter pulled aside the curtain across the doorway.

'Father's compliments,' he said. 'And will you come to his cabin, pronto.'

'Oh, lord! What's eating the old boy now?'

'Search me, Doctor. He's getting the Mate up there, and the Hunk.'

'Hunk?'

'Chief Steward, Mr. Whimble.'

'Very well.' I rolled off the bunk and took my cap from the hook over the desk. 'I hope it isn't his stomach again.'

Hornbeam and Whimble were already sitting on the settee in the Captain's cabin. McDougall was in one of the armchairs. On either side of the desk sat Captain Hogg and Mr. Montmorency, the Fathom Line's manager in Buenos Aires. All of them were smoking cigars and drinking liqueurs.

'Ah, Doctor, come in!' Mr. Montmorency called, as I pushed the door curtain away. He got up and seized me by the hand. 'Have a seat. Move over there, Mr. Whimble. Cigar? Real Havana. Won't find them in England, eh? Benedictine, Curaçao, or brandy? Some Kummel, perhaps? Or a flash of the old starboard light?'

'Benedictine will do nicely,' I said. I sat down between Whimble and Hornbeam, while Mr. Montmorency lit my cigar. He was a lean, brown man with a brisk black

F

moustache, dressed in a crisp linen suit. He was an office-wallah, and therefore formally despised; but he was secretly respected as an important and dangerous man in the lives of everyone who depended on the Fathom Line for their pay. Beneath the sunburnt hearty crust was a sharp brain eager to send damning cables to St. Mary Axe, where a few words of code could hold up a man's promotion for ten years or tip him back into the uncertain currents of the shipping pool. Even Captain Hogg was affable to Mr. Montmorency.

'Right, gentlemen,' Mr. Montmorency went on forcefully. 'I have asked you up here to-day for a particular reason, apart from having the pleasure of meeting you. Captain Hogg assures me, I am glad to say, that he thinks highly of your services under his command.'

'A very happy ship,' Captain Hogg declared. He swallowed half a tumbler of Benedictine and glared at the rest of us in defiance of contradiction.

'I am sure it is, Captain. Now, gentlemen, I am going to talk to you on a most serious topic. It is British Prestige.' He took on his smartest Chamber of Commerce manner. 'It is hardly necessary for me to trace the course of events in this bustling sub-continent since the cessation of hostilities—hostilities, gentlemen, in which the Company we represent suffered as grievously as any—but you will, I am sure, all appreciate that the interest of our Motherland in its affairs has increased rather than diminished, though in the face of severe and sometimes to us inexplicable, opposition. Some more Benedictine, Captain?'

'Thank you, Mr. Montmorency.'

'Pass the bottle round, gentlemen. As I was saying. The tail of the British lion has been severely put out of joint . . .'

He went on about the Old Red Duster, Free Trade, the Socialists, Nationalization, Hard Times, the necessity to pull together, put our shoulders to the wheel, steer a straight course, and not rock the boat. All of us were hazily wondering where the speech was leading him and uneasily contemplating our own guilty consciences. I nervously calculated the turnover in Easter's dockside pharmaceutical dealings, Hornbeam thought anxiously about his stevedores' presents, and Whimble was wondering how to account for the ham and two cases of tinned pears that had somehow vanished between Santos and the River Plate. But, if these skeletons were visible to the penetrating eye of Mr. Montmorency, he was not going to mention it. I suddenly realized he was saying '. . . there will, of course, be a running buffet and the best we can do in the way of drinks. It will give the British colony here a bit of an outing, reassure the local businessmen, send up the prestige of the Line, and, in a small way, that of the Old Country. Besides, gentlemen, it will fittingly usher in the New Year. Any comments?'

McDougall, who had fallen asleep, woke up at the words 'New Year' and blew his nose loudly.

'A very generous offer,' Captain Hogg growled. 'On behalf of my officers and crew, I should like to express my gratitude to the management.'

'Thank you, Captain. Now, gentlemen, you are the senior officers. You know my plans, and I expect you to make it a success. This dance on shipboard must be remembered in Buenos Aires as one of the events of the season.'

A dance on shipboard. . . . I saw at once Tissot's painting—matchwood decks, fragile rails, graceful bright brasswork; summery officers with downy whiskers, in

gold and blue and white; clean sailors, contented bands-
men, delicate ladies in sprays of frills; frail parasols
pirouetting beneath a canopy of the majestic ensigns of
half a dozen now forgotten empires. . . . Into this they were
going to turn the *Lotus*, tied up by a meat works.

The news of the New Year's Eve Dance fell upon the
ship's company like a heavy breaker on the beach,
overwhelming the minor ripples already set up by our
misfortunes in the Saratoga the previous night. Reactions to
the party differed sharply. Easter was frankly disgusted.

'I ask you!' he said, coming into my cabin and tossing
an armful of my clean laundry peevishly on the bunk.
'What a lash-up! Flags, fairy-lights, and ladies' lavatories!
Cor! I dunno what they think this hooker is. The *Queen
Mary* isn't in it.'

'Surely, Easter, after your experience on the trans-
atlantic boats you would welcome a touch of the atmosphere of a large liner?'

'What, on this old tramp? First-class smoke-room now,
that's different. All the nobs in there getting stinko, not
noticing you rook 'em on the measure. And slipping you a
quid or two to show 'em the way to some young bit's
cabin—discreet like. What are we going to get on this
old tub? Crowd of shore-wallahs looking for free booze,
that's what. Fat lot of good that is!'

'You may be able to interest some of them in the three-
card trick.'

He brightened a little. 'I might, that, Doctor. But
there ain't no flies on them round these parts.'

Trail was ecstatic. 'Have you seen this, Doc?' he called
to me the next day, waving a sheet of typewritten paper.
'Lists of guests. Take a dekko. Don't bother with this lot,
Ambassador, Bishop, and so on, asked but not able to

come. . . . Look here—Mister and Missus *and daughter*. Here again—*and daughters*. All the way down—*Miss, Miss, Miss*. Lovely grub! The ship'll be like a bloody harem by eight bells!'

'I don't think you ought to get over-excited, Three-o. The Misses are probably elderly ladies, pillars of the Mission, and the daughters will most likely be still in short frocks. In any event, you can be sure they'll be kept under strict supervision by their watchful parents on a ship like this.'

'Steady on, Doc! There's bound to be some nice bits of crumpet among them. I think I know this one down here, anyway. Used to work in the Company's offices on Corrientes.' He rubbed his hands. 'It's going to be an Happy New Year, and no mistake.'

Hornbeam was less enthusiastic. 'More work for the bloody Mate,' he said. 'Half the bunting's gone mouldy and the Bos'n flogged the canvas awnings in the Canaries last trip. How the hell can I get the boatdeck holystoned and painted in three days? I bet we're short of Scotch homeward bound on the strength of it, too.'

A state of despair settled on Whimble. The greater part of the preparations fell to him, and he was expected to account for everything issued from his stores from a crate of Scotch to a jar of Maraschino cherries. Tablecloths, fruit bowls, glasses, and silver came from half-forgotten straw nests in dusty crates stowed under hundredweights of flour, rice, tinned vegetables, and a case of Gordon's gin he had lost three voyages ago and had been anxiously cooking the bar books to replace ever since.

'Oh dear, oh dear,' he said, coming out of the store-room with his shirt stuck to his chest with sweat. 'Balloons they want now! Did you ever hear of it? I don't know what the office will say when we get home!'

The balloons were a whim of Captain Hogg's; he had taken an enthusiastic and forceful interest in the dance, and spent most of the day pacing up and down the boatdeck rearranging the deck furnishings and decorations.

'Mr. Whimble!' he shouted frequently. 'Mr. Whimble! Where the devil are you? I think the buffet would be better on the port side. Not so many flies. Get it changed over. What's happened to Mr. Hornbeam? Bos'n, take down number three awning and rig it abaft the funnel so the holes won't show. Mr. Trail, are you supposed to be in charge of lifeboats?'

'Yes, sir.'

'You aren't fit to sail a toy boat on a paddling pool. Get those ropes stowed properly.'

'Aye aye, sir.'

'Doctor!'

'Sir?'

'Flies, Doctor. The bluebottles from the meat works. They are a sanitary problem, are they not?'

'Yes, sir. Included in the syllabus for the examination in Public Health.'

'You are responsible for them. I don't want a damn fly on my ship by to-morrow night. Understand?'

'It's rather a tall order, sir.'

'That's your look out. Get some insect killer from Mr. Hornbeam. I don't care how you go about it, but there aren't to be any flies.'

'Very good, sir.'

I could find only enough insecticide for one spray-gun, and this I gave to Easter with instructions to pump it vigorously round the Captain every time he stepped on to the deck. This seemed to satisfy him. He left me alone

until the evening before the party, when he called a
conference of officers in his cabin.

'This is going to be a damn good party,' he began
sternly. 'The office expects everyone to enjoy themselves,
and it's bloody well up to you to see they do. Get me?
Now listen to this.' He picked up a sheet of paper from the
desk. 'These are the Master's orders for to-morrow night.
One: uniform. Clean number tens, with correct epaulettes
and white shoes. Collars to be correctly buttoned up.'
He glared at McDougall, who came to supper comfortably
in carpet slippers, with the high collar of his jacket wide
enough apart to allow the dragon tattoed on his chest to
peep coyly over his second brass button. 'Doctor, you will
wear white ducks, white shirt, black tie.'

'And Company's Regulation Cap, sir?'

'If necessary. Two: Guests are to be met at the head
of the gangway by Master and senior officers. See the
quartermaster's in uniform and sober, Mr. Hornbeam.'

'Aye aye, sir.'

'Three: No ladies are on any account to be entertained
in officers' cabins, or elsewhere than on the portions of the
boatdeck assigned for that purpose.'

'There goes Trail's evening,' I whispered to Hornbeam.

'Four: All alcoholic liquors on board to be placed under
seal at noon to-morrow and no such liquors to be served
to any member of the ship's company before the arrival
of guests at ten o'clock to-morrow night. Five: All shore
leave stopped from noon to-morrow. Six: All members of
ship's company to remain decent and sober throughout
to-morrow night. My ship is on show, gentlemen. Understand?'

We murmured acceptance of the terms.

'The music will be provided by a band from one of the

English clubs,' Captain Hogg continued. 'Get the Sparks to jack up the amplifying system in case we have to play records, Mr. Hornbeam. Have you been through the ship's record library, Mr. Whimble?'

'They seem to be sort of operas and stuff, sir.'

'Capital! I like a bit of opera. Right, gentlemen. Oh, Doctor, I've put that man of yours in charge of the bar.'

'Who? Easter?'

'Yes. Strikes me as a reliable honest sort of fellow.'

I swallowed. I felt any opinion of mine would spoil the contentment of both of them.

'Very well. Conference dismissed.'

As we went down the companionway together I said to McDougall 'The prohibition order's going to delay you chaps getting Hogmanay away to a good start.'

He dropped a red eyelid over a crafty eye.

'It'ud take more than yon pipsqueak to stand in a Scot's way on Hogmanay, lad. Come along to my cabin when you've finished yer tea to-morrow. We'll find you a dram or two from somewhere.'

15

I WAS called from my shower at eight the next evening
to put half a dozen stitches in the forehead of a fireman
who had fallen down the stokehold ladder. For this
reason I was the only officer who arrived on deck to greet
the guests sober. Captain Hogg's orders had been punc-
tiliously obeyed, except for the one impounding the ship's
supply of liquor; since tea-time Whimble had been
poking his head in his locker like a nervous ostrich in a
perilous desert, in the Chief Engineer's cabin Scots
accents rawed under the sting of neat whisky, Hornbeam
and the Mates poured gin from the water-bottles above
their basins, and Captain Hogg himself had been entertaining Mr. Montmorency and his sleek Argentine wife.

The boatdeck of the *Lotus* looked surprisingly attractive.
Fairy-lights shone on the fresh white chalk spread over
the scrubbed deck, ensigns and signal flags lined the rails
and obliterated the stark Frigorifico, and on the long
tables garnished with blazing Argentine flowers glass and
linen fell pleasingly and promisingly on the eye. The
band—three Argentines with piano, guitar, and drums—
was seriously tuning up behind the ensign of the Common-

wealth of Australia. At the head of the gangway, which was enlivened with bunting and a string of bulbs, a quartermaster stood nervously in white matelot's rig; stewards in shining jackets stood with silver trays and serviettes between the fresh-painted ventilators; behind the bar was Easter, with an expression of disarming honesty on his face that suggested a bishop going through the Dover customs with two bottles of brandy in his gyp.

Besides the quartermaster the ship's officers—in clean white number tens, white shoes, correct epaulettes, collar fully buttoned up—stood greeting the guests with great charm and affability. To me it seemed that the decorum of my shipmates had a certain brittleness about it, a nervous over-emphasis. This was noticeable in the way the Chief Engineer tenaciously kissed the hands of the ladies; the hesitation with which Whimble brought a match to a guest's cigarette; Hornbeam's roar of laughter; Trail, open-mouthed, mentally stripping every woman under forty stepping off the gangway; and the abandon with which Captain Hogg was pinching Mrs. Montmorency's bottom.

I felt a tug at my elbow. It was Easter leaning across the bar, holding out a long glass of brownish fluid.

'Best respects, Doctor,' he said hoarsely. 'This is the stuff I'm making up for me and my mates.'

'What is it?'

'Little cocktail I invented on the Western run. I calls it "Fire Alarm." '

'Thank you, Easter. I fancy I have some leeway to make up.'

The guests seemed to be shippers and senior Fathom Line employees who knew each other and Mr. Montmorency well, and were therefore relieved of the cumbrance

of social chatter while getting down to the free drinks and
lobster patties. As I was not in uniform no one bothered
to talk to me, and I was content to stay in the shade
of a ventilator by the bar, smoke the ship's cigarettes,
drink Fire Alarms, and leave the entertaining to my
companions.

'Ché, un cigarillo por favour.'

A slim brunette with incandescent eyes and teeth stood
in front of me.

'I beg your pardon?'

'Oh, don't you speak Spanish? I only want a cigarette.'

I handed her one from my own tin.

'Thanks. You work in the meat-works too, do you?'

I was hurt. The *Lotus* may have been a rusting old-
fashioned tramp, but that night I was proud of her.

'Not a bit. I'm one of the officers.'

'What of this old tub? You look too respectable. Why
aren't you dressed up?'

'I am the Doctor,' I explained stiffly.

Her eyes instantly shone brighter. 'Well, what do you
know? I get the most crippling pain in my back.'

I saw at once that I had committed a social error.
During my spell as a general practitioner I had learned
that members of the public meeting a doctor socially
believe they can entertain him only by briskly trotting
out an account of their illnesses. When introduced to the
bank manager they do not immediately start talking about
their overdrafts, and on shaking hands with the local
J.P. they are not compelled to discuss the number of
times they have been summonsed. But they firmly hold the
idea that the doctor can be diverted for half-hours at a
time by details of their symptoms, or even those of far-
away relatives and dead acquaintances.

'It sort of catches me round here,' she continued, twining her arm behind her and pushing her sharp bosom forward. 'Whenever I twist round suddenly—Ouch! See what I mean? I've been to doctors all over the world—London, Paris, New York, here in B.A. They never did me a bit of good, though. I still had my pain. Sometimes I woke up in the night and screamed.'

'Very distressing for you, I'm sure.'

'Oh, I began to lose faith in doctors. You don't mind my saying so, do you?'

'Not a bit. Have a Fire Alarm.'

'What is it?'

'It's a drink. Very good for backache.'

She giggled. 'Well, then I went to an osteopath in Wimpole Street—he was sweet. He told me I had a displaced spine. What do you think? He slipped it back again, like shutting a door. There!'

'I think that . . .'

'I only used to get it after that when it rained. Why do you think that was? And then I was playing tennis out at the Hurlingham Club last month, when Bingo! I . . .'

'May I introduce you to our Third Officer?' I interrupted. 'You will find him very charming.'

For the past few seconds Trail had been staring at my companion with his mouth open. He jumped at my remark so much he spilt his drink on the deck; then he stepped forward with the expression of a hungry deckhand going in for his Sunday dinner.

'Mr. Trail,' I said, 'Miss . . .?'

'Ella Robinson.'

'Mr. Trail is our most popular officer,' I whispered to her. 'The Captain thinks highly of him. But if I may speak as a shipmate, he is a little shy and needs encouragement. Enjoying the dance, Three-o?'

'Have another drink,' Trail said thickly.

'I think he's cute,' Miss Robinson decided, flashing him a swift glance of appraisal. I had been treating his spots since we left Santos, and in his clean white jacket and painstakingly Brylcreemed hair he looked as presentable as an Ian Hay subby.

'Har!' Trail said. 'How about a dance?'

'Mmm! I've never danced with a sailor before! Be a sweetie and hold my glass, Doctor.'

Grinning weakly, Trail drew her on to the chalked square of deck and began dancing with the spirit that nightly won him hearts in Reese's dance hall in Liverpool. I contentedly took another Fire Alarm from Easter and leant back on my ventilator. After the night at the Saratoga anyone so pressingly feminine as Miss Robinson was too much for me.

When the music stopped the couple came back to my corner of the deck. Both of them were flushed and breathless.

'You're a swell dancer,' Miss Robinson said to Trail, giving him a hot glance of admiration.

'Am I really?' he asked eagerly. 'Go on!'

'Yes, I mean it. Not like most Englishmen out here. When I dance with you I sure know I'm dancing.'

'Have another Fire Alarm,' I said, signalling to Easter.

'Do you dance, Doctor?' she asked.

'Definitely no. I come from a family with very strong views on the subject.'

'How amusing! Do you know, my pain's coming back. Look!' She turned round. 'Run your hand down my spine.

That's right—just there! Ooo! Exquisitely painful! What
do you think I ought to do about it?'

'I should go and see a doctor.'

She laughed playfully. 'Gee, you're funny! You're the
nicest doctor I've ever met.'

'Thank you. Down the hatch, now.'

We drank our Fire Alarms, and the band began to
play again.

'Let's dance,' she said to Trail.

'Not for a minute,' he said. 'Let me show you the
steering gear.'

'What on earth should I want to see the steering gear
for?'

'It looks most attractive in the moonlight,' I added
encouragingly. 'Not many people are privileged to see it.
Only Mr. Trail and the Captain have the key.'

'C'mon,' Trail said. He gave her a look that would
have terrified the heart out of any girl in England and
strode off purposefully with her, hand in hand, towards
the steel nooks and shadows of the stern. I moved to the
rail, leant over the strip of dirty, oil-coated water between
the *Lotus* and the quay, and exchanged glances with the
two sour Argentine policemen standing at the foot of the
gangway. The night was hot, and the awnings prevented
ventilation. Shortly the ship's officers unhooked their high
collars and wiped their foreheads with coloured hand-
kerchiefs, and sweat began to run down the faces of the
guests.

No one bothered me, so I sipped my way through my
drink and thought guiltily about England. I was inter-
ruped by 'A hundred pipers an' a'' from the corner
where the band had been playing. It was almost eleven-
thirty and the engine-room had by then taken over the

party for themselves. The engineers were lolling round the piano with an air of genial possessiveness towards every-thing they could see, and McDougall was stripped to the waist, his dragon, hearts, and sailing ship glistening among the grey tufts of hair that sprouted from his thorax and shoulders like bracken on a Highland hillside. Singing with them was Captain Hogg, drunk to the point of harmlessness, and the Montmorency's. The music was provided by Easter, who was playing the piano in the style of Chico Marx.

With a flourish Easter finished his piece, rose to his feet, and announced solemnly, 'Ladies and Gentlemen, for my next number to-night I shall give you my rendering of the famous old English ballad "The Lily of Laguna."' Jolly good luck to you, gentlemen, jolly good luck!' He sat down heavily and began the tune, to which most of the audience sang the words of 'Annie Laurie.' McDougall then shouted it was midnight by ship's time as the clocks were to be advanced half an hour, and broke into Auld Lang Syne. This was taken up by the company, and I was swept into a chain of crossed hands. McDougall sang with his eyes tightly shut, swaying between a pair of other Scots; suddenly he stopped, shouted 'Kiss all the lasses!' and dived towards Mrs. Montmorency. He grasped her in his moist naked arms and kissed her hotly until he was elbowed out of the way by Macpherson, MacPhail, and Macintosh. These were followed by Captain Hogg, Easter, Whimble, one of the Argentine policemen from the dock, the Quartermaster, Hornbeam, and myself. Then everyone sang Auld Lang Syne all over again.

At the end of the verse Captain Hogg shouted 'Eight bells! Quartermaster, ring eight bells! Midnight, ship's time!' Mrs. Montmorency instantly threw her arms open,

and was kissed by McDougall, Macpherson, Captain
Hogg, McDougall again, myself, Easter, Hornbeam,
McDougall once again, Macpherson, MacPhail, and
McDougall. She appeared to enjoy these unstinted
tributes thoroughly, though Mr. Montmorency, who
stood fidgeting beside her, was moved during her fourth
embrace with McDougall, to murmur nervously, 'Steady
on Maria! I say, steady on, old girl!' We sang Auld Lang
Syne and kissed Maria Montmorency several times, as a
member of the circle recalled that it was midnight in
Greenwich, Glasgow, Greenock, or some other point of
overwhelming importance to himself. Finally her husband
grabbed her by the arm and led her to the gangway
while everyone cheered and Easter played 'Sons of the
Brave.'

The engineers and Hornbeam then decided to visit the
Taxi-Dance on the other side of the dock.

'Come on, Doc,' Hornbeam urged. 'It's only over the
ferry. We can get there in ten minutes.'

'I thought you hadn't any money?'

'I flogged some whisky to the policeman. It's a cheap
joint—the girls will darn your socks as well for twenty pesos.'

I shook my head. 'No thanks. I've got into enough
trouble in B.A. already. Besides, I'm tired. I'm turning in.'

I left my shipmates, who were already on the gangway
with bottles sticking out of the pockets of their white
ducks. I was tired and muzzy. Easter's Fire Alarms had
an effect like anæsthetic ether, producing a disturbing
numbness and inco-ordination of the extremities; all I
wanted was to lie on my bunk, turn on the forced draught,
and sink on to the soft foam that overlies the dark cool
liquor of unconsciousness. Yawning, I unhooked my cabin
jalousie, pushed the curtain aside, and turned on the

light. On the deck was Trail, asleep; two half-empty whisky bottles and some broken glasses were on the desk; lying on my bunk, her skirt round her waist and snoring heavily, was Ella.

I began with an attempt to resuscitate Trail by throwing the remains of my drinking water over him. From this it was apparent that he was in a state of deep surgical anæsthesia, and I could have cut a leg off without his noticing it. While I was shaking him and slapping his face I heard a deep groan from the bunk, and noticed that Ella was wearily moving her arm. I dropped Trail and began flicking her face with the end of a towel. She shook her head and muttered something.

'Ella! Ella!' I called. 'Wake up! Come on—for God's sake, woman! What's that?'

I bent my ear close to her.

'Wanna be sick,' she said.

'Oh, lord!' I lay the towel over her, poised my empty hot-water can on her bosom, and hurried down to the hospital to find some sal volatile.

When I came back she was sitting on the edge of the bunk, her head held heavily in her hands, her long black hair scattered uncaringly over her shoulders and forehead, her eyes closed, and her face white. She looked like a patient at the end of a long operation.

'Here! Ella! Drink this,' I said cheerfully.

She pushed me away clumsily.

'Don't wan' another drink.'

'This isn't drink—it's medicine. Make you feel better, see? Jolly good stuff. Look! I'm having some myself.'

'Wanna go home.'

'Yes, I know. But drink this first. It's something special.'

'For Chrissake take me home. For Chrissake.'

'Oh, all right then. Where do you live?'

There was a pause. She slowly shook her head.

'Dunno.'

I looked hopefully at Trail, but he seemed unlikely to take part in any conversation before noon the following day.

'Ella,' I said gently. 'Think please. Where do you live? Haven't you got a phone number?'

'Wanna go to bed.' She started to roll back on my bunk, but I caught her.

'No, you can't go to sleep,' I told her firmly. 'There'll be hell to pay if I don't get you out of my cabin and off this ship. Now try and remember where you live. The street will do.'

I spotted her handbag wedged down the side of the bunk, opened it, and found one of her visiting cards. It bore an address in the Palermo district, which I thought was somewhere on the other side of Buenos Aires.

'All right,' I said, slipping my arm under her shoulders. 'We're going for a walk.'

The gangway quartermaster gave me a grin.

'Lovely grub, eh, Doctor?' he said. He winked and smacked his lips, in case I had missed the point of his remark.

'Benson,' I said sternly. 'I need about two hundred pesos. I should be obliged if you would lend it to me, if you have it. I see no prospect of repaying you until we return home, but if you refuse I shall give you hell should you happen to fall sick on the voyage back. Thank you.'

We stumbled down the gangway together, Ella grasping my collar and groaning. After picking our way over the railway lines and bollards on the quay we reached the little office of the dock police by the gate. I gave the policeman ten pesos and asked him to call a taxi; twenty minutes later we were bumping along the dirty road beside the Frigorifico, Ella already asleep and snoring on my shoulder.

The cab stopped outside a tall block of flats several miles from the ship. I gave Ella a shake, and she woke up with a start.

'You're home,' I said. 'End of the line.'

'Oh God, I feel horrible.'

'So do I.'

'Take me in . . . Please!'

'Can't you make it yourself?'

She shook her head.

'Oh, all right then.'

I helped her out of the cab, making signs to the driver to wait. We went into a small hall, which contained a staircase and an automatic lift. As I opened the lift doors Ella leant heavily on my shoulder and burst into tears.

She told me, through sobs, she lived in number seventeen, on the third floor; the key was in her handbag. I took her up to her own door and opened it. At that moment her knees gave way. She began to slide slowly down the doorpost.

'The room opposite,' she muttered. 'For God's sake help me in.'

I supported her across the hallway and into the room opposite the flat door. I turned on the light with my free hand, and found I was in her bedroom.

'Put your arm round my neck,' I commanded. She obeyed, and I lifted her up, laying her on the bed heavily.

'All right,' I said. 'You can unclasp my neck now.'

I heard a noise behind me and turned. Standing in

the doorway was a tall, stern, greying gentleman with a stiff moustache and a military eye, dressed in a yellow silk dressing-gown. Behind him was a timid, sandy, becrackered woman in a faded housecoat.

'I've a damn good mind to horsewhip you,' the grey gentleman said decisively.

'Now look here, I say . . .' I began.

'I might tell you I consider you an unmitigated cad. I've no idea what your upbringing is, but I don't imagine it's very savoury. If I were a few years younger I'd give you a good hiding with my bare fists. A young puppy like you needs teaching a good lesson.'

'Be careful, Charles,' the woman said nervously. 'You know what you did to the Rolleston boy.'

Charles twitched his muscles under his dressing-gown. Ella seemed to have Bulldog Drummond for a father.

'I should never have let her go on that damn ship,' he said bitterly. 'I believed at least the officers would be gentlemen. I was mistaken.'

'Mind your temper, Charles,' the woman added timidly, covering her eyes with her hands.

'Now, look here,' I said angrily. 'I assure you I have had nothing to do with your daughter . . .'

Charles snorted. 'Pray, how do you explain that lipstick all over your shirt? A disgusting exhibition! By God, I'm not at all certain I shan't horsewhip you after all . . .'

'Charles, Charles!'

'You have got quite the wrong end of the stick . . .'

Charles by now had time to look at me carefully and find I was much smaller than he was. He advanced, going red in the face.

'Put them up, you young hound!' he growled.

There was nothing for it. I threw one of Ella's pillows at him, sidestepped quickly, and dashed for the door. I shot into the lift, leaped for the taxi like a survivor grasping for a lifeboat, and drove back to the ship, looking nervously through the back window at every turn for cars bearing greying gentlemen in silk dressing-gowns, who were anxious to relieve the strangling monotony of Buenos Aires' social life by avenging the honour of their daughters. And when I got back I found Trail had recovered sufficiently to climb into my bunk.

16

I SPENT the rest of our time in Buenos Aires walking the broad, criss-crossed, sun-drenched streets looking for a cheap watch. I kept out of the bars, and if I thought a woman looked at me I jumped.

The momentum that had carried us headlong into the pleasures of South America had expended itself by the end of the dance; afterwards our lives settled into the unexciting routine of a ship in port. Every morning I read carefully through the English *Buenos Aires Standard*, had a cup of tea with Hornbeam, and strolled round the active decks; in the afternoon I filled my cabin with the last squirts of our D.D.T. spray and slept soundly until tea, in defiance of the rattling winch just beyond my head. Now and then I picked up *War and Peace*, but the freezing plains of Russia seemed so fantastic I killed a few cockroaches with it and finally put the books away for the voyage home.

In the evening, when the sun had gone down and a breeze sometimes blew off the River Plate to refresh our decks, we sat in Hornbeam's cabin with a case of tinned beer playing sober games of bridge or liar-dice. I felt that

I had been living alongside the wharf in Buenos Aires for a lifetime, and I sometimes stared at the familiar angles of my cabin in disbelief that they had ever been softened with the shadows of an English winter's day. When I told the others this one evening Hornbeam said: 'You'd get used to living in Hell, Doc, if we sailed there. All these places are the same, anyway.' He lay on his bunk half-naked, fanning himself with a copy of the *Shipping World*. 'They're hot and sweaty, and full of blokes ready to cut your throat for tuppence. It's the same out East and on the African coast. There's no more romance at sea than there is round Aldgate tube station.'

'When are we leaving for home?' I asked.

He shrugged his shoulders. 'I couldn't say. Maybe a week, maybe two. It depends how the cargo goes in. Once you're in port the wharfies have got you, whether it's in Cardiff or Calcutta. I heard from the agent to-day the boys might be cooking up a strike. That would fix us, right enough.'

'I wouldn't mind a pint of old English wallop out of the barrel just now,' Archer said seriously. 'Or a bit of backchat with a Liverpool barmaid. You can have too much of these high-pressure floozies out here.'

We sat looking miserably into our beer glasses, all suddenly homesick.

'I reckon I ought to have married and settled down,' Hornbeam continued. 'I nearly did once. I'm still engaged to her, if it comes to that. She's in Sydney. Sends me letters and sweets and things. I see her about once every two years.'

'I should have stuck to selling refrigerators,' Archer said to me. 'I did it for a bit after the war, but I had to give it up. Your money doesn't go anywhere ashore these days.'

'You fellows don't know how well off you are in the Merchant Navy,' I told him.

'The Merchant Navy!' Hornbeam said, folding his hands on his bare stomach reflectively. 'It's a queer institution. A cross between Fred Karno's army and a crowd of blokes trying to do a job of work.'

'There's no security at sea,' Archer added gloomily.

'Maybe it's better than sitting on your fanny in an office till you drop dead,' Hornbeam said. 'Pictures every Saturday night and Margate for a fortnight in summer. Drive me up the pole, that would.'

'Margate's all right,' Trail remarked, joining the conversation. 'I knew a girl who lived there once. Her father ran a shooting-alley in Dreamland.'

17

IT was a fortnight before we sailed. A quiver of excitement ran through the ship with the fresh vibrations of the engines. The deckhands ambled about their work singing—not sea-shanties, because they heard those only occasionally, on the pictures, but anything they knew from 'She'll Be Coming Round the Mountain,' to 'Rock of Ages.'

'All hands seem to be pretty happy,' I observed to Easter as a man sauntered past chanting 'Every turn of the screw brings me nearer to you.'

'Well, we're going home, Doctor!'

'But we've only been away a couple of months.'

'Still, it's always like this, whether you've been away two years or a fortnight. You gets a bit slap-happy when you leaves your final port.'

'I think I can understand it. For most of them I suppose it's only an attic in Liverpool or a dirty old house in the East End.'

'Still, it's home, sir.'

'You're right. Where do you live, Easter?'

'Down in Cheltenham.'

'Do you indeed?'

'I lives with the old lady,' he continued. 'She keeps a sweetshop down there. Getting a bit past it now, though. Well over seventy.'

The idea of Easter having a mother was disturbing. I had thought of him vaguely as climbing out of the sea on the heels of Venus.

'Are you coming back next trip, Easter?'

'I suppose so,' he replied. 'I've tried it ashore. Done all sorts of jobs. Apart from the halls and the races, I've worked in pubs, laundries, hotels, fish-and-chip shops. Even done a bit of navvying. Sometimes I gets settled into something steady, but . . . well, you know how it is. I goes round to the public library and has a look at Lloyd's List on a Saturday afternoon, and I'm finished. I think how nice it would be getting away somewhere instead of standing in a queue in the rain.'

'I'm afraid I see your point, Easter. But perhaps you'll get married?'

'What, at my time of life? And after what I've seen of women? Cor! I've had 'em all, I have—black, white, brown, and yellow. They'll all the same underneath.'

'Do you read Kipling, Easter?' I asked with interest.

'Kipling? He's dead now, ain't he?'

'He doesn't seem to be dead at sea.'

'No, I don't read much, Doctor. No time for books. Takes you all your life to keep going these days, don't it?'

We detached ourselves from the meat works and steamed slowly down the long buoyed channel along the shallow River Plate towards Montevideo and the Atlantic. From there we had a straight run home, broken only at the Canary Islands for oil. The sea was calm and the sky unbroken. Off Montevideo we left the last persevering

seagull behind us and were again alone, ourselves and the
sea.

'About another three weeks,' Hornbeam said, 'and
you'll be having a pint at the Carradoc.'

'I hope it turns out cheaper than the last drink I had
with you.'

He laughed.

'Remind me to get you a new pen, Doc. Anyhow, we
ought to have a pretty quiet voyage till we reach the
Bay.'

And so we did. Two days out Captain Hogg became
more morose than usual, then took to keeping to himself.
For a few days he came down to meals, which he consumed without passing a word or giving any indication
that he sensed our presence at the table at all. As no one
else dared to speak this meant that lunch and supper were
eaten in a silence that amplified such noises as chewing a
stick of celery to the volume of a Tropical thunderstorm.
After that he took his meals in his cabin, and appeared
only occasionally on the deck. He would stand outside his
door for a few minutes, scratch his head, blow his nose,
and disappear for the day. Everyone was delighted.

'The Old Man's got a proper cob on about something,'
Hornbeam said. 'Never pokes his nose on the bridge.
When I go to his cabin he just grunts and says he's left
the running of the ship to me. Suits me fine. Life's nice
and quiet, isn't it?'

'Yes, it's wonderful. I wonder how long it'll last?'

It lasted until the night of the shipwreck.

When we were two days away from the Canaries the
weather broke suddenly, within a few hours. The sun was
intercepted by heavy English-looking clouds, and a cold
wind came down from the north and threw handfuls of

rain across our decks. I lay in my bunk, rocking contentedly and confidently in the swing of the ocean. It was
shortly after midnight, and I was suspended in the
pleasant arcade between sleep and wakefulness, enjoying
the best of both. Then the alarm bells rang.

I sat up and switched on the light. Seven short rings,
meaning 'Boat Stations.' Someone on the bridge had
obviously leant on the alarm button. I was wondering
what to do when the whistle blew 'Abandon Ship.'

'Christ!' I said. I jumped from my bunk like a sprinter
off the mark. I fell over the hot-water can, picked myself
up, and threw open the cabin door. Trail lived opposite
me, and had just come off watch. He was looking disturbed.

'What's up?' I asked anxiously.

'It's abandon ship.'

'I know! But why?'

'Search me, Doc. She was all right when I came off the
bridge. We'd better get up top.'

I hitched up my pyjama trousers and started for the
companionway.

'Your life-jacket, you fool!' Trail shouted at me.

'Oh lord! I forgot.'

I ran back to my cabin, pulled on my life-jacket, and
started tying it. It occurred to me I should make an
attempt to save some of my possessions, so I picked up my
empty sponge-bag and stuffed one or two handy articles
into it. I later discovered I had preserved from the deep a
shoehorn, two empty cigarette tins, a roll of film, and a
copy of *Teach Yourself Spanish*. Grabbing a tin of morphine
from the locker, I hurried towards the boatdeck.

The crew of the *Lotus* had boat drill at four-thirty
every Friday afternoon, as prescribed by the Ministry

of Transport, and this was always carried out efficiently, with calmness, and in an atmosphere of polite co-operation. There are, however, certain factors that complicate boat drill in earnest which are not operative during its harmless rehearsals. In the first place, it is usually night-time, there is a cold wind blowing, and it is raining. A strong sea is running, which makes it difficult to swing the boats out without smashing them. Everyone has been woken up from a deep sleep and is bad tempered. The Bos'n has forgotten where he put the handle to one of the davits. The Third has lost the roll-call. All hands are perplexed and naturally worried about saving themselves as well as giving wholehearted enthusiasm to preserving their shipmates. Also, all the lights are out.

I slipped over the wet deck, now alive with hurrying sailors, and found my way to the huddle of men round my own boat. They were cutting away the strings holding the canvas cover, under the directions of the Third.

'My God, what a lash-up!' the Third said. 'All right, Bos'n. Stand-by to swing.'

'Swing out all boats!' Captain Hogg's voice came through the loud hailer.

'Swing out!' the Third repeated.

Three men swung on each davit handle with an energy usually shown at sea only when arriving in port ten minutes before the pubs shut.

'Swing out, there!' Captain Hogg repeated. 'The ship is going down!'

A rocket flew into the air and exploded into gently falling coloured stars.

'Get a move on, you men!' he shouted.

'Come on, come on!' Trail ordered impatiently. 'Stand-by the falls, there!'

'Excuse my interrupting,' I said. 'But if we're sinking we don't seem to have much of a list on.'

'Cut it out, Doc! Right, lower away there! Steady, forrard!'

Hornbeam, in his life-jacket and underpants, came breathlessly over to us.

'What's up?' I asked.

'Search me. The Old Man started it. I went up to the bridge and he kicked me off.'

Suddenly the deck lights snapped on. We all paused and looked at one another.

'Right!' came from the loud hailer. 'That was the poorest exhibition I've seen in all my years at sea. That was boat drill, see? As it should be done. None of this Friday afternoon tea-party stuff. You're the most inefficient crew I've ever had the misfortune to sail with. Swing 'em in again and dismiss.'

To a chorus of groans and ingenious profanity the boats were swung in and made fast.

I went below to change my clothes and pour myself a drink. I was still towelling myself when Trail came in.

'What the hell does Father think he's up to?' he demanded, throwing his wet life-jacket on my bunk.

'I suppose he's allowed to hold boat drill at night if he wants to.'

'He's allowed to, all right. He's allowed to do anything. He can marry you, bury you, put you in irons, or hang you from the yardarm. That doesn't mean to say he can do it every night.'

'What do the crew think of it?'

'They're complaining to their Union.'

'I wish I could complain to mine.'

Trail pulled his wet jacket off and sat down. 'I wonder

what made the Old Man do it?' he asked more calmly. 'It's the first time we've seen him for a week.'

'Probably didn't want us to forget him.'

'That's likely. It's finished with now, anyway. It was bloody cold up there on deck. You're going to have about twenty pneumonia cases to-morrow.'

'Care for a peg before we turn in?'

'Thanks, I'll have a quick one.'

I was handing him the whisky bottle when the whistle blew for the second time.

The scene on the boatdeck was repeated, but it was played at a much more leisurely pace. The crew showed no enthusiasm at all for the exercise.

'Come on!' Trail ordered. 'It's got to be done, so you'd better get it over with.'

'Put your backs in it!' the loud hailer roared. 'Call yourselves sailors? Get a move on with number four, Mr. Trail!'

'For God's sake, lads,' Trail said. 'Keep the Old Man happy.'

Slowly our boat swung out, rocking in the wind, tugging at the arms of the swearing crew.

After twenty minutes on the cold, wet deck, Captain Hogg gave the order to swing in again. The boats were brought back to their blocks, lashed down, and covered with their canvas sheets.

Hornbeam, who had found time to put on his uniform, came back to us.

'All squared up, Third?' he asked anxiously.

'Aye aye, Mr. Hornbeam.'

'All right. You lot can dismiss.'

The voice came from the loud hailer.

'Right! Now repeat the exercise!'

Hornbeam spun round.

'No!' he shouted towards the bridge. 'We won't!'

The wind and sea were making a fair noise, but these were obliterated by the silence that fell upon everyone on deck. I held my breath. The bridge was in darkness, but I imagined clearly the explosive figure standing there.

The loud hailer was still for a few seconds.

'This is mutiny!' it roared.

Hornbeam shrugged his shoulders.

'Dismiss, all hands,' he said. 'Disregard all further alarm signals.'

'Mr. Hornbeam, I'll put you in irons!'

Hornbeam took no notice.

'You'll pay for this, by God!'

'You see everything's lashed down, Third,' Hornbeam continued calmly. 'I'm going on the bridge.'

He made towards the ladder.

'You come up here and I'll kick your teeth in!'

He reached the end of the ladder. A heavy fire-bucket fell on the deck, just missing his head. I got hold of him and pulled him away.

'Look here,' I said. 'Don't be a fool. Let me go up and see him. After all, I'm more or less out of this. I can explain it's bad for the crew on medical grounds, or something. He's got nothing against me. I can be an intermediary.'

'Nothing doing, Doc. This is my pidgin.'

'No, it isn't. I don't want to spend the rest of the night putting stitches in your scalp. I'm sure he won't chuck anything at me.'

'All right, Doc,' he said. 'But watch your step.'

Setting my teeth, I climbed up the ladder to the bridge. At first I thought the wheelhouse was empty. Then I caught sight of the Captain, standing by the terrified quartermaster who was steering. He looked like a fat malignant ape.

'Who's that?' he growled.

'Doctor, sir,' I began. 'I came on behalf of the Mate . . .'

'Get off my bridge!'

'I wondered if I might explain that on purely medical grounds . . .'

'Get out!'

'In my professional opinion,' I continued resolutely.

'Get out!' he screamed. 'Or I'll bash your bloody brains in!'

He seized from the bulkhead some heavy instrument. It was, I suppose, a marlin spike or some similar appliance that skippers are traditionally expected to take to beat in the brains of their crew. I did not wait to find out. I scrambled down the ladder and fell hard on to the deck. I hurt my arm and ripped my pyjamas; but already I had forgotten the incident. A new and more terrifying thought took possession of me: Captain Hogg was undoubtedly clinically insane.

18

'Delusions of grandeur,' I read aloud, 'occur frequently in this condition.'

It was the next morning. Hornbeam and Trail were sitting in my cabin while I read aloud from a text-book of medicine. The weather had calmed down and the storm that blew through the ship the night before had abated with it. Immediately after turning me off the bridge Captain Hogg had abruptly gone to his cabin, locked the door, and turned in. He appeared in the morning without making any reference to the night's excitement, and was even faintly friendly towards everyone on board. He gave the impression that he imagined the activity on the boatdeck was part of a particularly enjoyable dream.

'You see,' I explained to the others, 'delusions of grandeur. I ought to have spotted it before. Still, it's difficult in a ship's captain. No one notices if they have them.'

'What's wrong with him, Doc?' Hornbeam asked with interest.

'G.P.I.—general paralysis of the insane, undoubtedly. It's a late stage of syphilis. Listen to this: "The patient is usually a man in his middle fifties who suddenly becomes subject to attacks of bad temper, fits of sulking, and lack of judgment. These may alternate with periods of violent excitement. The condition is usually first noticed by members of the sufferer's family circle rather than the physician." Doesn't that fit in? The old boy picked it up thirty years ago on the Brazilian coast and now we're getting the benefit of it.'

Hornbeam rolled a cigarette thoughtfully.

'It's a serious business, Doc, if you're right.'

'I'm pretty certain I am.'

'Is there any sort of test you can do to make sure?' Trail asked.

'I couldn't give you a definite opinion without examining him.' I ran my eye down the page of the book. ' "The patient has the sensation of walking on cotton-wool," ' I read out. 'Stabbing pains in the legs at night . . . loss of knee-jerks . . . loss of pain sensation in the tendo Achilles . . . pupils do not react to light . . . There's a good many signs, you see.'

'Yes, but do you suppose he's going to let you barge into his cabin and examine him?' Hornbeam asked. 'Have you thought about that?'

'You raise a difficulty in diagnosis, certainly,' I admitted. 'I don't feel he would be a highly co-operative patient. Particularly after last night.'

'Well, we'll have to let him go on being balmy, then.'

I shut the book and took my spectacles off.

'I have an idea,' I announced. 'I remember the way I was once told to examine children.'

'Children! This one's some baby!'

'It's the principle of the thing that matters. They

taught us in hospital to deal with unwilling children by distracting their attention and examining what you wanted while they weren't looking. See what I'm getting at? The knee-jerks, for instance. I shall engage him in conversation and drop a book or a bottle of something on his patella, pretending it's an accident. Oh yes, I think that's the answer,' I said, warming to the idea. 'I'll build up a diagnosis in a couple of days and send in a report to the Company.'

'Mind he doesn't bite you,' Trail said.

I had a chance to try my new technique of fragmented diagnosis at dinner. Captain Hogg appeared for the first time since his retirement, and seemed in capital spirits. He sat down next to me at the head of the table, tucked his serviette in with a flourish, and fell upon the roast mutton.

'Good mutton, this, Mr. Whimble,' he said through a mouthful of potatoes. 'Don't get much like it these days. Where did you buy it?'

'London, sir.'

'It's kept well. By the way, Mr. Hornbeam. Get the hatch covers off number three by to-night, if the weather holds. We may be filling that twenty feet in Teneriffe.'

'Very good, sir.'

'I'm pleased to find the weather's cleared, sir,' I said brightly. 'This fresh breeze makes you feel you're walking on cotton-wool.'

He said nothing.

'Do *you* ever feel you are walking on cotton-wool, sir?' I asked.

'No,' he said. 'I don't.'

He swallowed another mouthful of greens and mutton. I was keenly disappointed.

'The weather ought to hold,' he said. 'The glass is going up.'

'I had an aunt,' I remarked. 'Every time the glass went up she had stabbing pains in her legs.'

'Did she?'

'Do *you* get stabbing pains in your legs, sir?'

'What the devil are you talking about, Doctor?'

'Oh, nothing of importance, sir.'

I miserably fiddled with a piece of roast potato. It seemed that my means of eliciting the patient's symptoms was not going to meet with clinical success. I decided I would go ahead and examine for the physical signs. I dropped my serviette on the deck. As I bent down to pick it up I pinched Captain Hogg hard behind the ankle.

'Ouch!' he said.

'I'm dreadfully sorry, sir . . .'

'What the hell are you playing at?'

'I thought . . . I thought it was the Mate's foot.'

'Well, what difference does that make?'

'We were having a little game.'

'I don't like games,' Captain Hogg said. 'Not in *my* ship.'

'Very good, sir.'

I jabbed moodily at my treacle sponge for the rest of the meal, despair freezing my heart.

'Find anything out?' Hornbeam said in my cabin afterwards.

'Not much. Couldn't you see?'

'Yes, you were making a bit of a mess of it. Supposing he's not potty at all, but just acting his own sweet self?'

'I'm *sure* he's insane,' I said heatedly. 'Certain of it. If they put him in the final examinations every student would get through. He's a classical case. The only trouble is I can't get near enough to prove it.'

'We'll have to be pretty certain before we say anything to the Company, Doc. I always believe in clearing my own yardarm.'

I banged the desk with my fist.

'Damn it! Here's this man—certifiably insane—with every one of us at his mercy. Why, any time he might break out again like last night! Supposing he goes and puts us aground at the Canaries? Or rams the *Queen Mary* or something off Bishop Rock? He's capable of absolutely anything. What would we do then?'

Hornbeam scratched his cheek with the lip of his pipe.

'It's a teaser, Doc. We'll have to think out some other scheme.' He looked at his watch. 'I must go and tell the Bos'n to take the covers off number three. If I think of anything, I'll let you know. Meantime, I'll keep a sharp watch on Father myself.'

'Thanks. I'll try and work something out. See you for a peg before supper.'

I passed the rest of the day sorting ingenious schemes for diagnosis in my mind. Nothing seemed workable. I thought of confessing frankly to the port doctor in Teneriffe that we had a madman loose on board and asking him to send for a couple of assistants and a strait-jacket; but I felt that the port doctor, who was used to ship's captains, might find Captain Hogg not in the least abnormal. I wished sincerely that he would foam at the mouth or do something equally spectacular when we got in.

When Easter brought my tea I admitted my difficulties to him.

'I think the Captain is insane,' I told him.

'Ho, yes,' he said. 'He's as mad as a fiddler's bitch.'

'You've noticed it too, have you?'

'Dr. Flowerday always reckoned he was.'

'Did he do anything about it?'

'Used to slip the cook half a dollar to lace his tea with a Mickey when he was real bad.'

'I hadn't thought of that. It might do in an emergency.'

'Wasn't much cop, as it happened. He chucked the tea at the steward usually.'

'We must think of some way, Easter, to settle this once and for all,' I said firmly. 'I am prepared to give you ten bob—a quid—if you can think of some legal means of getting the Captain off this ship at the first possible moment.'

Easter scratched his head.

'Very kind of you, Doctor, I'm sure. Can't think of anything offhand, like.'

'Well try, man, try. If I can't think of . . .'

I was cut short by a crash outside my cabin, a loud scream, confused shouting, the clatter of running feet.

'What the hell's happened now?' I exclaimed.

My door flew open. Hornbeam was outside. He was grinning like a tooth-paste advertisement.

'Quick, Doc!' he said. 'Father's fallen twenty feet down number three hatch!'

I ran on to the deck. There was a crowd round the edge of the hatch, hurriedly letting down a rope-ladder. I pushed my way through and climbed over the combing. In a few seconds I found Captain Hogg had solved all our problems for us by fracturing his right femur in three places.

*   *   *   *

Easter and I strung up Captain Hogg in splints on his bunk. He was a heavy man, and still not a remarkably co-operative patient. It took us a couple of hours, and we were sweating when we had finished.

'I'll have that Bos'n logged,' he muttered, as we arranged the pillows under his head. 'Leaving the covers loose like that . . . I'll have the Mate logged, too.'

'Now keep quiet,' I commanded. 'I forbid you to talk or move.'

'I will talk as much as I damn well like.'

'I give the orders now. I'm the doctor.'

'Well, I'm the Captain.'

'Easter,' I said. 'Just tighten up that splint a bit more, will you?'

'Ouch!' said Captain Hogg.

'Now,' I continued. 'If you will just stay quiet for a moment I can complete my examination. If you don't I shall have to consider putting you on a milk diet. Tinned milk, naturally.'

I pulled out my torch and shone it in his eyes.

'Ah, yes,' I said, in my most menacing professional tone. 'As I thought. Just take this down, Easter. Pupils do not react to light . . . loss of sensation to pinprick over the nose . . . abdominal reflexes absent . . . A classical picture! We will have to put you ashore to-morrow in the Canaries, of course.'

'You will not. I am not leaving my own ship for you or anybody.'

'Damn it, man! Use your sense. This leg has to be set properly. I can't do it here. It needs X-rays and so forth. You will have to go into hospital with it. I hear they have some excellent surgeons in Teneriffe.'

'I will not go, Doctor.'

'If we cable the Company and they say so, you'll have to go.'

'There is no reason why you should cable them. I am still fit to keep my command.'

'It's a bit late to think of that now. The message has already gone.'

'Gone!' He jerked his head from the pillow. 'No messages are allowed to leave the ship without my permission.'

'Really, you are a most difficult patient,' I said gently. 'I will leave Easter to read to you. You will find plenty of literature in the corner, Easter.'

'What, these here?' Easter asked, picking up one of the Captain's library. 'Cor! Looks like a bit of all right, eh?' He settled himself comfortably by the sick-bed. 'Right, sir,' he began. 'I will start with "I was a White Slave. True Confessions of a French Girl Kidnapped from a Convent and Sent to the Infamous Kasbah of Algiers." Cor,' he added to the Captain, 'I know Algiers all right. Funny thing happened to me last time I was there. I'd gone ashore with the Cook, see, and we was looking for a bit of fun, as you might say . . .'

I left them, feeling I had inflicted on Captain Hogg sufficient misfortune for the evening.

Hornbeam was sitting in his cabin writing up the log-book.

'Hello, Doc,' he said cheerfully. 'How's the patient, God rot his soul?'

'As well as can be expected, I'm afraid.'

'I'm just putting it in the log. You'll have to sign down here.'

'When will we get to Teneriffe?' I asked.

'About midday. We should be tied up alongside by one.'

'We've got to put Father ashore, you know. I can't treat a fracture properly at sea. The trouble is he won't shift. He says he won't go without instructions from the Company.'

Hornbeam tossed a cable across to me.

'Sparky just brought that down,' he said. 'Take a look at it.'

I unfolded the paper. It was from the Fathom Line head office.

TO CHIEF OFFICER SS. LOTUS, it said. PLACE CAPTAIN ASHORE TENERIFFE IF DOCTOR SO ADVISES AND BRING VESSEL HOME UNDER YOUR COMMAND STOP PREPARE TAKE COMMAND IMMEDIATELY ON ARRIVAL UK SS PRIMROSE OWING RESIGNATION CAPTAIN BARSETT.

'Well, Doc,' he said smiling. 'Do you advise?'

'Do I advise! Yes, sir! Yes, indeed!' I grabbed his hand. 'Yes, Captain Hornbeam!'

19

THE next day we arrived off the rocky, volcanic Canaries, sailed under the lee of the islands and shortly after noon slipped into the tidy, clean harbour of Teneriffe. Archer and Trail took the bow and stern, tugs flying smoky red-and-yellow Spanish flags turned us round to face the sea, and we tied to the jetty between a smart Blue Star boat outward bound for Rio and a disconnected-looking craft flying the flag of Panama which had cows on the deck.

At first Captain Hogg refused to be moved. We showed him the cablegram but he accused us of forgery. So I filled him up with morphine and sent him to sleep.

He was carried out on the shoulders of the sailors, like Nelson's bier, arranged in a derrick sling, and unloaded by the steam winches between two bales of cowhide.

'You'll find the full history in the letter,' I said, handing the case report to the smiling, handsome Spanish doctor with the ambulance. 'The British Consul's fixed everything else up.'

The doctor shook hands, the ambulance doors swung

shut, and Captain Vincent Hogg drove out of my life.

'Get rid of him all right?' Easter asked, as I reached the top of the gangway.

'It seems so. I don't think he'll have much chance to throw his weight about in a Spanish hospital. Especially after that letter I sent with him.'

'Wouldn't mind going ashore here for a spell myself,' Easter said meditatively. 'I've had some fun here, I have. I remember when I was on the South Africa run, the barber and me went . . .'

'All right. Easter. Later will do.'

'They got some lovely girls here,' Easter continued. 'Prettiest in the world, I reckon. Look at that one down there. See? They got the same as our girls at home, but they carry it around better.' He pointed to a slim, dark girl, stepping along the quay with a grace that is unhappily forgotten on cold English parks and pavements.

'Ho, they got some smashing bits here!' Easter said enthusiastically. 'Mind you, you've got to be careful. Do you want a tablecloth?'

'A tablecloth? What should I want a tablecloth for?'

'This is the place to buy them.' He pointed over the side, where the wide pipes ran towards the ship in a pool of black fuel oil. An informal market had been set up on the quay, offering thick brocaded tablecloths, scarves with vivid bullfights on them, canaries in cages, metal ornaments, and dolls four feet high.

'Them dolls is all right,' Easter advised me. 'I used to buy a lot of them at one time.'

'I'm pleased to hear you think of the children, Easter.'

'Ho, crikey no! I used to buy 'em here and flog 'em in

Pernambuco. Good business, that was. Canaries, too. Make a good few bob on canaries, you could. Unless the little bastards went and died on you. Or you got gyped. Some of 'em's sparrows fed on quinine.'

'Well, I ought to buy a few presents, I suppose. But I haven't got much in the way of money.'

'They takes all kinds of junk here. Old clothes—a pair o' boots, worn out, if you've got 'em. Fags mostly. Get anything for a few hundred Woods.'

I exchanged five hundred ship's Woodbines for two scarves, a small bracelet, and a decorated picture of General Franco. I supposed I had better make a return with some of the assets of a seafarer.

We stayed eight hours in Teneriffe; then we set off under Hornbeam's command, our next stop England.

The removal of Captain Hogg from the ship had the effect of dissolving a chronic state of anxiety. All hands walked about cheerfully, did their work amiably, and set to it with twice the effort.

'Got to have her looking nice for home now,' the Bos'n said, looking critically at the gang he had set painting the upper works. 'We can't let Mr. Hornbeam down, can we?'

Hornbeam slipped easily into his new rank. He took over the Captain's cabin and his seat at table. Our mealtimes now were lively with conversation, with the result that everyone ate more contentedly and the cases of dyspepsia among the officers dropped sharply. Even Archer began reluctantly to feel better, and admitted he hadn't taken any stomach powder for a week.

Our only excitement was a message to Hornbeam changing our destination from Liverpool to London because of a threatening dock strike. The order caused disapproval among the Liverpudlians in the crew, but this was charmed away quickly by Easter's account of the fun he had had at various times in London.

'Smashing place, London,' he claimed. 'You wait till you see West Ham.'

The sea became rougher, the weather became colder; spray came once again over the *Lotus*'s bows. The broken water took on the green-grey tint of European coasts, and the ship began to groan and stagger in the January waves. But now I was unaffected by the sea, and stood on deck innocuously watching the foc's'l head rise and dip with the swell and the tops of the masts trace wide irregular circles against the sky. All round us were signs that we were coming nearer to our own country. Boxes and cartons were lying in everyone's cabins, the ship's time became synonymous with that of Greenwich, three pounds Channel money was advanced to all hands, the Light Programme assailed us undiminished, and the weather remained persistently foul.

One evening Easter put his head round my door and said cheerfully 'Want to see the Ushant light, Doctor? Just coming up on the starboard bow.'

Together we stood in the shelter of the storm door leading on to the deck. I followed his finger towards the flashes.

'Well, there's old Europe again,' Easter said. 'Ain't a bad old continent, all things considered. We turns the corner here. The next mark's the Casquettes, then for Beachy. Blimey, I've seen folks in tears looking at that there light! When they've been gone for a long time, that is.'

'Yes, I expect everyone will start being excited from now on.'

'Ho, they'll have the channels to-morrow, you mark my word.'

'The channels?'

'Ah, there's a complaint what even you don't know, Doctor. All hands goes a bit balmy, like. You wait till to-morrow.'

Easter was right. The channels is a clinical entity that has not found its way into the medical text-books, but is as noticeable as scarlet fever. The next morning the crew were prancing round the decks like highly-strung lambs in springtime. Everyone had a bright word for their mates, a salute for the Captain, and even a few sirs left over for me. Work was done with a lighthearted air that drew scowls of disapproval from the Bos'n, who had been up the Channel so many times that he had developed an immunity to the complaint. Easter repeated his most successful card tricks and thought it a great joke to tell me falsely the hospital was three feet in water. I forgave him readily, for I too was walking the deck murmuring to myself, 'Every turn of the screw brings me nearer to you.' To whom? I wondered. It didn't matter. I could settle that when we arrived.

Beachy Head—white, shining in a brief ray of sunshine turned on like an effective spotlight on a darkened stage. I looked at it with mixed feelings of affection and disapproval that the voyager's first sight of England should be Eastbourne.

We came closer to the land, making for the pilot boat off Dungeness. The Atlantic rollers had flattened themselves in the narrow waters, but the sea was high enough to throw the pilot's launch about unenviably. He came round to the lee side and had two shots at grasping the Jacob's ladder Trail and the Bos'n dangled from the foredeck; the third time he caught a rung as the launch dropped away from his feet. He climbed aboard, his black oilskins running with water, shook himself like a dog, gave me a cheerful 'Nice morning!' and climbed up to the bridge. The red and white pilot's flag broke over the wheelhouse, and the *Lotus* proceeded under the arrangement invariably stated in the log-book as 'Master's orders, Pilot's advice.'

The Channel was busy that day. We passed, or were passed by, a representation of Lloyd's List. There were tankers making for Thameshaven, so low in the water they disappeared to the bridge between the waves; rickety tramps setting out fearlessly for voyages longer than ours; little coasters bound for a rough passage round Land's End; sodden fishing boats; cargo ships of all sizes and states of repair, British, Norwegian, Swedish, and Dutch; one of the ubiquitous City boats with a black and salmon funnel, homeward bound fully loaded from the Australian wool sales; even a couple of warships. They were a pair of corvettes steaming jauntily down Channel in line astern. The meeting led to a burst of activity at the foot of the mainmast as the deckboy afforded the King's vessels their salute by dipping our ensign. The correct form was for us to dip, watch for the white ensign fluttering down in reply, and follow its return to the masthead. Unfortunately, the wind caught our rain-soaked flag and twisted it in the rigging, so that we passed the fleet apparently in mourning. But the intention was there, and the Navy would be the first to understand.

A big white P. & O. passed us, outward bound for India and Australia and the sunshine that appeared to me to have vanished for ever,

'Be away for the best part of four months, that lot,' Easter remarked. 'All be taking their last look at old England.'

'As long as that?'

'They gets them dock strikes something horrid out Aussie way. It's a lovely life being a wharfie in Sydney or Melbourne—you draws your money and puts your feet up most of the day. Like being a lord. Or—if I may be so bold—ship's doctor.'

'Yes, I suppose you're right,' I admitted sadly. 'Except the dockers get paid more. I suppose they're all pretty excited on board—first night at sea, and so on.'

'Ho, yes. I've seen it often enough on the big passenger boats. All the blokes giving the girls the once-over in the dining saloon. Cor, I've seen them sweet little things with their eyes still wet with tears from saying good-bye to their husbands and sweethearts carrying on something shocking. Hardly out of the River we wasn't, neither.'

The red lamps were shining on the tops of the high radar masts when we crept close to Dover inside the Goodwins. The lights of Ramsgate and Margate passed off our port side, then we cut across to the Nore, where we were to anchor and await the tide. Someone gave me the morning paper that the pilot had brought aboard. I opened it and read the front page with the careless baffled interest of a holidaymaker inspecting the social column in the village weekly. We had been more or less newsless for three months, but the happenings that used to shake my breakfast table no longer aroused my concern. A paragraph near the foot of the page caught my eye; it was headed 'MAYOR REBUKES DANCERS,' and went on: 'The Mayor of ——, Alderman ——, yesterday refused an application for an extension to midnight at a cycling club dance. He said he was highly disturbed at complaints of immoral behaviour that had followed the dance last year. "The place for young men and women at midnight," he told the secretary, "is in their own homes asleep." '

I knew I was back in England.

20

THE next morning we steamed into the Thames. The country raised a faint glow of sunshine to welcome us, but the effort was too taxing and the atmosphere soon relapsed into its habitual rain.

We passed the long finger of Southend Pier, which appears a far more dignified structure when seen in reverse, signalled our name, and passed down the channel towards Tilbury. The wet, orderly fields of England on the narrowing banks, with a demure English train jogging through them towards London, had the appearance of a winter's garden after the turbulent unfenced vegetation of the South American coast. Off Tilbury landing-stage we anchored for the Port of London doctor to board us. He was a large, friendly man in a naval battledress and a duffle-coat.

'Have a good voyage, old man?' he asked, running his finger down the pages of my log-book.

'Pretty good, thanks.'

'Going again?'

'Oh, no. I don't think so, anyway.'

'Back to the N.H.S., eh?'

'That's it. If I can remember any of my medicine.'

He laughed. 'You can still sign your name, can't you? All right, free pratique granted.'

We continued down the River, and I was seized with a spasm of nostalgia by catching sight of an L.P.T.B. bus.

In Gallions Reach the tugs set about us and turned us towards the locks of the Royal Albert Dock.

'Is that all the room we've got?' I asked Easter, as we headed for the narrow entrance. As I always had difficulty parking a car in a busy street I filled with admiration for the mates and tugmasters every time the *Lotus* came into port.

'There's bags of room,' Easter said. 'They gets them big New Zealand boats through here easy enough. Look at all them bright lads we've got to help us.'

I saw a chilly knot of longshoremen waiting to receive our ropes as we came into the lock: sad, damp Englishmen, their coat collars up to their sodden caps.

'That one there's been on the job for years,' Easter said. 'We calls him Knuckle 'Arry.'

He pointed to a depressed-looking man with a long moustache standing still and holding a rope fender over the end of the jetty.

'That's an odd name. What's his knuckles got to do with it?'

'The knuckle's what he's standing on. Now you wait.'

As the *Lotus* drew near the stonework the pilot shouted from the bridge: 'Keep her off the knuckle, 'Arry!' The man touched his cap, and solemnly manipulated his fender to save our paint. He then resumed his immobility in the thick rain.

We passed the knuckle, the locks, the entrance to the dock; the tugs dragged us slowly down to our waiting

berth; more men in caps and old overcoats secured our
ropes to the quay; the ensign came down from the gaff
and was rehoisted, in compliance with custom, on the
stern jack-staff.

'Lower away gangway!' Hornbeam shouted from the
bridge.

The *Lotus* leant contentedly against the dock and, after
three months all but five days, we were home.

*   *   *   *

There was a wonderful end-of-term spirit abroad.
Everyone was packing up and behaving with the reck-
lessness of men for whom there are no longer any
consequences.

We were paying-off, the morning after our arrival. Mr.
Cozens and his colleagues came aboard and treated us
with cordial superiority, and we looked on them with
good-humoured contempt. Cozens himself questioned me
closely about the exit of Captain Hogg.

'Very good, Doctor,' he said. 'I think you did entirely
the correct thing. Our *Sunflower* is due at Teneriffe in
three weeks' time and she will bring him home. We have
your successor for next trip—a Dr. Gallyman. Do you
know him?'

'I'm sorry, I don't.'

Cozens sighed. 'I'm afraid he is a little on the old side,'
he said. 'Retired from practice some years ago. I believe
there was some trouble with the medical authorities,
too . . . Still we must hope for the best. It's so difficult
getting doctors for these ships just now.'

Apart from the office staff, the ship filled with taxi-
drivers, luggage carters, laundrymen, dry cleaners,
marine tailors, and haircutters, all of them pressing their

services on the ship's company before it dispersed. I shut the door of my cabin, looked despairingly at the empty cases and my curiously augmented possessions, and wondered how I was going to pack. I started with the volumes of *War and Peace*. I hadn't got beyond the first page, but I had killed one hundred and thirty-two cockroaches with them. I was hesitantly fitting them into a case when Easter came in.

'Letter for you, Doctor.'

It was only the second one I had received since leaving Liverpool. It too was from the laundry.

Dear Sir, (it said) '*Further to ours of November* 28*th. I have to inform you that your laundry has been sold to defray expenses of the wash. The sum received was* 6*s.* 3*d., which is* 1*s.* 9*d. less than your account. We would appreciate your settling this deficit at your earliest convenience.*'

Sadly I put the letter into my pocket.

'Getting the loot packed, Doctor?' Easter asked.

'I only wish I could.'

'The Customs is pretty hot down here,' he went on. 'Not like some ports I could mention. Get away with murder, you used to. So long as you bought your tickets for the police ball.'

'What police ball?'

'I remember once the old arm of the law putting his head round our cabin door and saying, "I'm sure as you gentlemen would like to come to the police ball." Well, I knew the ropes, see, so I says, "Not 'arf we wouldn't. We've been thinking about it all voyage." So he hands over tickets at a dollar a time—but you mustn't take 'em, like. I looks at mine and says, ' "Ho, constable, I regrets but what I have a previous engagement." So he collects all

the tickets back and flogs 'em again in the next cabin.
Mind you, he keeps the five bob.'

'Well, I hardly think it worth while my making the
investment. Apart from the junk I got at Teneriffe I've
only some corned beef and a pair of nylons.'

'That's the ticket, Doctor! Girls round our way will
do anything for a tin of corned beef. Show 'em the nylons
as well, and cor! they're all over you.'

'I assure you these are destined for middle-aged
relatives.'

'Used to do pretty well out of nylons during the war.
Some of the blokes on the Western Ocean made a fortune
flogging 'em in Southampton. The places they thinks of
to hide 'em! Down the chain locker in the fo'c'sle's usual.
One of the lads put a dummy pipe across the deckhead
and filled it with nylons and fags. Lovely job he made of
it. Painted it up just like it was real. But the Customs boys
copped him. Oh, they're very fly, they are. I'll get you
an empty beer-case from the Chief Steward.'

'Thank you, Easter.'

I sat wearily among the disheartening jumble. Well,
this was the end of the trip. What had I got from it?
Some corned beef, some nylons, a cure for headaches, two
stones in weight, and a deep sunburn. But much more
than that, surely I had found for the first time that the
world isn't divided simply into two classes—doctors and
patients. Three months at sea had taught me more than
six years in a medical school. I had learned to give and
take toleration, to grapple with grotesque predicaments,
to appreciate there is some goodness behind everybody, that life isn't really so serious, and that doctors
aren't such bloody important people after all.

The Customs man—young and keen—came in and

rummaged my cabin. He did so like an old-fashioned physician searching for a diagnosis with an irritating air of professional detachment.

'Where did you get these from?' he asked, holding up my best pair of pyjamas.

'Swan and Edgars.'

'Umm. Have you any spirits?'

'Bottle of whisky.'

'Opened?'

'Certainly.'

'Umm. Have you a watch?'

'No.'

'What, not one at all?'

'I lost it one night in B.A.'

He looked at me narrowly.

'Watch your step, Doctor,' he said, leaving me alone.

I managed to throw my packing together before paying-off started in the saloon. It was more a ceremony than a business transaction. We were theoretically not entitled to any pay until the end of the voyage, though we could draw foreign currency at the pleasure of the Captain. Our wages were set out in a long narrow sheet, with additions for leave and Sundays at sea and deductions for advances, Channel money, bar bill, stores account, and anything else the Chief Steward thought he could add without protest.

The pay was distributed by the Fathom Line officials, under the eye of the Shipping Master. They sat at the big table behind exciting piles of five-pound notes, looking like the tote about to pay off on the favourite. Also on the table were the ship's articles and a pile of discharge books—the sailor's personal record—signed by the Captain with a comment on conduct like a school report.

The crew lined up eagerly, all in their best clothes. I had difficulty in placing the clean, modest-looking men in smart blue and grey suits as the half-naked roughs who strode round the decks with paint pots in the Tropics. The Carpenter was particularly baffling: he wore a dark herringbone tweed, a hard white two-inch collar, and an artificial rosebud in his buttonhole, giving the appearance of a moderately liberal-minded clergyman on holiday at Sandown.

Nothing gives such a pleasant feeling of false prosperity as paying-off a ship. By the time my wages had been reduced by deductions I had less than a month's salary in general practice, but I stuffed the notes into my pocket and felt like Lord Nuffield. Then I signed off the book of ship's articles opposite the space where I had signed on them three months ago. My contract with the Commander of the *Lotus* was broken: I was quit of my obligations to him to obey his lawful commands, to work the ship in emergency, to abstain from bringing my own liquor on board, and to check myself from using foul language in his presence. For his part, he had no longer to trouble about feeding me at the required standards, avoiding carrying me into Arctic or Antarctic latitudes, and return-ing me to my own country within a period of eighteen months. I was free—out of work, but free.

I said good-bye to as many of the crew as I could find; sailors farewells are brief and shallow, for they make up half their lives. Easter shook hands heartily and impressed on me solemnly the importance of speed whenever I should come to do the three-card trick. Almost everyone left the ship—to go on leave, to quit her for good, or to be in Canning Town by the time the pubs opened. The rain prevented cargo being worked, and the *Lotus* was not only empty of people but silent, as miserable as a school when the children have gone home.

My taxi was coming later, so I went up to the deck to look round the docks. The sheds and the cranes did something odd to the *Lotus's* proportions: at sea, when she was alone and stood unhindered from the water, she achieved a touch of dignity. Now that she lay in relation to other pieces of wood and steel she shrank and became ridiculous. The long boatdeck I used to walk was hardly the size of four railway waggons, and the enchanted spot where I sunbathed and watched the flying fish in the afternoon was nothing but a sooty piece of wet planking. Standing in the rain I saw clearly, but with regret, that the land is ever master of the sea.

I saw Hornbeam, in his blue raincoat, striding alone up and down the few feet of shelter below the bridge.

'Hello, Doc,' he said as I went up to him. 'You off now?'

'In a few minutes. I'm only waiting for my taxi.'

'Oh well, I'm sorry to see you go. We haven't had a bad voyage on the whole. We've made a bit of fun for ourselves.'

'We certainly have.'

We walked for a minute or two in silence.

'What are you going to do now, Doc?' he asked.

'I've no idea. Find a practice somewhere, I suppose.'

'Do you reckon you'll go back to sea again?'

'Some day I will. I'm making sure of that.'

'You might, at that.'

'How about you?' I said. 'Going on leave?'

'No leave for me, Doc. I'm off to Liverpool to-night to join the *Primrose*. She's sailing to-morrow for New Zealand.'

'Of course, I was forgetting. You know, to me our arrival is the end of an isolated adventure. But I suppose to you and everyone else it's just another stop in port.'

'That's it, Doc. Always on the move. It's a mug's life, isn't it? Still, someone's got to do it.'

My taxi came then. I waved to him from the dock, and watched him as I drove away. He was walking up and down the deck again in the rain, an incongruous and lonely figure.

*   *   *   *

The first person I went to see in London was the psychiatrist.

'Hello!' he said. 'When are you going away?'